MW00335011

Hecate

WITHDRAWN

WITHDRAWN

$\mathscr{H}$ECATE

The Adventure of Catherine Crachat: I

PIERRE JEAN JOUVE

TRANSLATED BY LYDIA DAVIS

T$_M$^{P}

THE MARLBORO PRESS/NORTHWESTERN

EVANSTON, ILLINOIS

The Marlboro Press/Northwestern
Northwestern University Press
Evanston, Illinois 60208-4210

Originally published in French in 1928 under the title *Hécate*. Copyright © 1962 by Mercure de France. English translation copyright © 1997 by Lydia Davis. Published 1997 by The Marlboro Press/Northwestern. All rights reserved.

The publication of this work has been made possible in part by a grant from the National Endowment for the Arts. The costs of translation have been met in part by a subvention from the French Ministry of Culture.

Printed in the United States of America

ISBN 0-8101-6038-2

Library of Congress Cataloging-in-Publication Data

Jouve, Pierre Jean, 1887–
      [Hécate. English]
      Hecate / Pierre Jean Jouve ; translated by Lydia Davis.
            p. cm. — (The adventure of Catherine Crachat ; 1)
      ISBN 0-8101-6038-2 (alk. paper)
      I. Davis, Lydia. II. Title. III. Series: Jouve, Pierre Jean, 1887–
      Adventure of Catherine Crachat ; 1.
PQ2619.O78H3813 1997
843'.912—dc21
                                                                97-18100
                                                                CIP

The paper used in this publication meets the minimum requirements of the American National Standard for Information Sciences—Permanence of Paper for Printed Library Materials, ANSI Z39.48-1984 .

Contents

WHAT I AM

I

Some time ago a trivial "adventure" befell Catherine Crachat. Catherine "Spit"—quite a name, isn't it? A name that could only be borne by a creature of grief.

Catherine Crachat was on a train arriving in Paris from I don't know where—from Basel, or from Marseilles. Catherine Crachat is very beautiful. She had been on the train all night, but this happened in second class, and no one was pretty to look at. Nevertheless, there were two men in Catherine's compartment. One of these men (strong, dark-haired, energetic, I clearly recall) had not closed his eyes since the train started, so as not to miss anything of drowsy Catherine.

No one on the platform for Catherine; a movie actress coming back from filming in the mountains or by the sea, such people don't have anyone waiting for them at the station. Catherine jumped down onto the platform with her long legs, briskly, and immediately disappeared. The gentleman with the dark hair had tried in vain to follow her. Catherine bore away with her a regret or, shall we say, an odd feeling.

A quarter of an hour later, in a line of blocked cars in the rue de Rivoli, the dark-haired gentleman found himself next to her, each of them in an unmoving taxi. Well now, isn't that odd. In the sunlight he appeared to be a good, intelligent, ordinary sort of person. She averted her eyes so as not to "knock him dead," but, perceiving the man's aggressive delight, she knew that she was already having a strong effect on him. The gentleman's taxi was sticking closely to hers, so she gave several contradictory orders to her driver and managed to lose the love-smitten man (since she herself felt nothing). The fact is, in any case, that she is hardly given to facile love. And this must be pointed out before the rest of the story is heard: Catherine is generally cold where pleasure is concerned, very cold, except in the circumstances of the true love she has positively known, and even in those circumstances she had required a sort of grace. She is not maternal and is not accustomed to being tender. Anyhow, she is not one to reap pleasure from her unkind behavior; yet for her there is virtue in suffering and in stirring the suffering in herself and in others, for is it not by this damnable path that one proceeds toward purification?

Even so—she felt absolutely on the verge of yielding to the dark-haired gentleman.

At four o'clock, as she was smoking a cigarette on her warm balcony above the street (this was in summer), she had the sensation (the desire) that she was hearing the traveler speaking down below with the concierge, Mme Pouche. She bent forward. At night she went and *deliberately* sat down on the terrace of a café on the nearby boulevard. And naturally she saw the dark-haired gentleman appear and settle next to her.

Catherine asked him his name, and what he said was: "I'm supposed to spend the evening at the home of a friend of mine. Would you like to go with me? We'll end up getting to know each other." They went to the home of a very distinguished lady living in the avenue de Valois whose name is Marguerite de Douxmaison. She identified him as her cousin or something like that. There they observed each other and brushed against each other for an hour or two. Then she took him back to where she lived. They talked, while drinking tea, about travel, about the stock market, and about family feelings. After that she did some rather coarse things with this man until morning.

However, Catherine Crachat's conception of life is not at all what you might attribute to her on the basis of this story; you should know that she had no positive reason for acting this way, and no *interest* in doing so. She was already, at that time, in mourning for a very great and altogether unique lost love.

I am Catherine Crachat.

Why introduce myself by way of a triviality? No reason. Hard to say. I find that such a silly adventure shows a person true to life, or at least a part of her, don't you think? Temperamental, unsure of herself, and unhappy, also shameless, that's certainly me. Wait till you know more about it. When we look back at the life we have led—or dragged behind us—what we see is the indictment of many hearts; and so I am beginning with myself! And then, is it so solidly established, is it as solid as they say it is, this world where "certain things are done and certain things are not"? That is how it was that I took this upright family man and got him to display his debauchery. When the challenge presents itself nakedly in my mind, it is a terrible temptation, I find nothing preventing me from going as far as I like.

I assure you that the next day I was as intact as I had been the day before, I mean I did not feel degraded by any of it, I felt pure in that place where I make the effort to be, in the soft, dark region of *me*. I have demons and also a fire for burning them. Fire! To set things afire—that was the idea that excited me when I was little! I still love to make something burn, see something burn. Stories about being burned at the stake frightened and entranced me. I would think about them to help myself fall asleep.

Well, the fact is I tried to burn myself with my own hands. When you're born as I was, with a frightful background, when you're made up of opposites, when you disguise yourself in order to live, and when you act a part with yourself and you're full of impulses violent to the point of savagery, and of fears, and of sorrows, when you're so sensitive you cry out (everything that touches your skin hurts) but nevertheless maintain a continual defensive stance, and when you're surrounded by shadow—in sum, by darkness—without anyone close by with whom to console yourself, without a guardian angel, when you're professionally beautiful, when you have a name that inspires disgust, in contrast to yourself, who inspire something else, when you're a movie actress and good for almost nothing—when you're Catherine Crachat.

I have been all of this.

II

I give you the impression of a rather easy enigma. Let's say it more plainly: I'm an adventuress. Even a tart, you will say. But take care, for certain people like to draw disrepute down upon their heads, and disrepute is the easiest thing to obtain. If you're old, you want to sleep with me—there, crudely, isn't that the sign of a man's real interest in a woman, which every woman aspires to elicit? If you're young, you shrug your shoulders, your square shoulders, the way they're wearing them these days: you find stormy women tiresome. There are moral people who will turn their backs and religious people will pity my soul. But no—I'm not that woman at all, nor the other one, nor any of those; I'll tell you. I'm a child who wants to cry. I'm a creature without hearth or home. I live, like everyone else, surrounded by luxury and stuff. But I'm not wicked. If you've seen me on the screen, you know that my finest roles have been brokenhearted little girls. I was born *deprived* and destitute, and for a very long time I didn't even understand what it was that I lacked. I loved almost no one. I lived in poverty. One time, though, I was happy; and right away it was only to experience worse privation. A thing passed over me like a divine breath, which would have raised me above my condition. I don't have it anymore, and yet again I do not understand why.

For a time, the gift of myself that I could offer furnished my life with a meaning. For otherwise my life is absurd, a juncture of all sorts of miseries. Oh, don't think I'm being too modest; I am

Catherine Crachat. That's a lot; it's a misfortune. I may possibly tell you about the thing that happened to me and that allows me to continue to survive. Sometimes I feel like talking about it to someone, anyone. But for everyone it's banal.

Do you know the rue Jacob up by the Hôpital de la Charité? It's dismal. That's where I live, I've been living there for ten years. Yet, there's the other side: my fourth-floor apartment looks out on a big walled-in garden. It is deeper than it is wide, and its tall chestnut trees put their lofty branches into my hand when I'm at my window. It's my garden. I still love it despite what it has done to me, but sometimes I can't endure it. There are four little fountains in the corners, an old bit of a private house opposite, with blue shutters, and in a window on the first floor a woman without clothes on is always combing her long hair. I loved with a passion the strange, miserable silence of its four walls, a silence traversed by the rumblings of automobiles.

The rue Jacob and all that, it's old now, it doesn't count for anything anymore, it has become transparent with time. You don't notice you're there, between getting off a train and boarding a steamship. I liked that. I travel a lot. But these days what sadness lays hold of me when I go back there! There are no words to express it to you. To such a degree that in the rue de l'Université, for instance, when I'm driving my car and I sense the house coming, I'm capable of turning to the right and to the left and going off somewhere, anywhere at all, like an idiot, or of stopping not far away for a half-hour or two hours, occupied with thinking whether I will go back there or not. For a while it was a disease. Some women, friends of mine, caught me playing this game and made a fine noise about it in order to add to my reputation as an eccentric! In the end I go back. The maid opens the door for me; as in the old days, as in the old days. I could die. Sad to the point where sadness is a kind of happiness, I stretch out on my bed and fall asleep, refusing to eat.

7

All of that is the echo of events whose theater was my room overlooking the garden.

Certainly, with all the traveling I have done, shouldn't I be able to forget the garden and those events that did not last even two years? I tried to change lodgings, and I had to come back here. When I was in Venice (in *The Death of Wagner*) where I had the Palazzo Vendramin to myself, I dreamed day and night that I was looking into the garden; I worked in London for a long time, and I would roam around in streets of brick blacker than mourning, but it would still be the garden. Everywhere I was Catherine Crachat or "Catharina" or whatever it might be, I played my roles, in straitened circumstances or with money, and I tried to like the new sky; but I stayed in the garden. What for me occurred *before,* the somber dream of my childhood and my adventures and my career and my dissipation, that's one thing, and that thing had to lead me—given what I am!—to the story of the garden. What happened there had to happen there. And the rest of my life, which was added *afterward,* glides over without changing anything and merely erodes sorrow through friction.

I think I will tell it to you, my story.

But first—I said I was beautiful. I know it's true. I'm beautiful by profession. Don't repeat it to me because I'm deaf from hearing it. Beauty is another misery you have to bear. When you have it along with a certain intelligence, you are unhappy. I would like to owe my life and position to something else. The phrase that declares to me that I'm beautiful truly offends me. "I have very sensitive black eyes, the oval of my face is full and regular, I have a marvelous mouth, dark hair with glints of steel, it can be fluffy, it can take on a scalloped shape, it can cleave close to my head; I am the new beauty between woman and man, supremely photogenic . . . etc." They sell pictures of me on postcards. And I also bear my name, which I didn't want to change, which I have only dimmed behind my first name, for the screen. Catharina. It's in bad taste, romantic. I have the same feeling of horror at my name and at my picture. I have to put up with both of them.

I'm looking for a man who is also a tomb. However, I will tell him only a small piece of the story. Do you want to be that man?

III

Between twenty-five and twenty-six, I had all my youth. I lived alone in that apartment, overlooking that garden. As yet I had no money. An old cleaning woman was my company. I was courted by the whole world; I didn't open my door. The maid took the bundles of flowers and the letters and put them on the mantelpiece.

But Paris, with its dog's life, work every day, my attempts at self-control, and a certain success in the career I was embarked upon, had done this poor unhappy girl some good. I had calmed myself and acquired a little self-assurance, I was going through an hour of respite.

Out of curiosity about pleasure, I had known a few men. It would end right away. I didn't believe in it. Aside from my sprees I would be alone in the house, on Sundays as on weekdays. An orphan not looking for friends. *I had paid my way* (as they say in English) in every sense, but this was so much better than the earlier nightmare! And because I was mimicking another's passion, it pleased me not to have any passion of my own. My heart knew the tricks light can play; and then, in my sprees, I didn't completely let go. I worked hard, I had engagements, and I was going to become a star of the second or third magnitude—"what I am."

In the house on the far side of the trees, there was a painter's studio. It was at my eye level. I am curious and I like poking around in other people's lives. My glances would reach in through his window. But he must have been a little higher than I was, and

9

when there was no foliage separating us, the painter could see me in my room, which made me wary, for I have a horror of being seen. The painter, a young man with a beard, was painting some sort of modern picture, and that's all I knew about him.

But some crates and flowers in some vague flowerpots on his little nothing of a balcony touched me, impossible to say why, but infinitely. Whom was I dreaming of? Myself. And that was the beginning. One day—it was the necessary day, there is always a fatal moment, a day, there was a day when Tristan heard tell of Queen Isolde for the first time—one day in early spring people were beginning to open their windows and I was resting in my bed. I was listening to the birds. They were going on and on, as though this were not Paris but the bank of a great American river, for example, in the midst of nature. What birds! Yes, one day. And ever since that day I cannot bear to lie facing a window.

They had somehow modified the glass in that window, or was it because of the midday sun? From my bed itself I was looking into the inside of the studio. It was very brightly lit. As though in a dream. The painter was at work. Nothing there to affect me one way or another. Between the back of the studio and the balcony (whose French window they had also opened) was the painter's model.

The position given to the model caused the model to look at me.

At first I trembled, I received the sort of shock you get when you enter the cold sea. When I saw just what it was that I was looking at, it was already too late. What brought me back to the feeling that I should defend myself was that shivering, which did not leave me. I was gazing at a slender, energetic hand resting on a knee and wearing a glittering ring. A tall young man, very blond, of an extraordinary race. He's like an angel, I said to myself. And I closed my eyes.

As I opened them again, the thought came to me that I was in my bed—my chest pretty much uncovered, no doubt; and that he was seeing me in my bed. He was indeed seeing me in my bed with my chest uncovered. I rang for my maid with all my might and shouted to her to close that window. This was my last act of resistance. I dressed. I appeared at the window. I was thinking only of him. I was him, and nothing else. I saw him again. He was just then standing up. He was looking at my window and the woman in the window. We said to each other, merely by closing our eyes, by opening them again, an obscure thing, a capital thing. No one caught us at our wiles: a meeting here the next day at the same hour.

It was thus that I came to know Pierre Indemini.

The next day I kept watch at the door of the painter's house. I saw the young man immediately. I said to him: "It's me. I like you. I love you. . . . Do you love me?"

"Yes, of course I do," he answered in the most beautiful voice in the world.

I cried out my name to him and I fled as though I were never again to see him on this earth.

"Mademoiselle, I don't know if you are real or unreal, nor whether what is happening . . . well, anyway, I can't allow myself to imagine. But I know that we have always been in harmony. Mademoiselle, I am so in love that I feel perfectly calm for the first time. I don't want to make a movement toward you. I want to wait. From having seen you and seen you only for one minute, I have the feeling of eternity. I feel an absolute confidence in you and in myself. I humbly embrace your knees. Pierre Indemini." This is his first letter. The following evening. Isn't it beautiful? And look at the writing, how noble it is. Strong and subtle, this writing aroused me like the hand that had traced it. I carried the true sign of his love against my breast. For, as yet, all I knew of him was his light hair, his tall stature with his broad but gentle shoulders, a certain nonchalance about his body, and I couldn't remember his features. As splendid as the young men in the frescoes in the old churches, and why not an angel?

IV

For our first meeting, I chose Jack's.

You've been to Jack's, it's a Negro dance hall. I would go and drink there when I couldn't stand my life anymore. On the ground floor of the cabaret they've blocked up the windows. A ventilator drives out the smell of sweat, and people dance in twos or threes. I had filmed a movie there once; I went back there, for that zigzag of Negroes and tall mannequins right up against your face; after two in the morning the women take their clothes off. The blues I found in that place were so incomparable, so absolute, so above me, that I savored a sort of peace.

I go in with him. I go in.

I went in leading Pierre Indemini!

I hadn't said a word to Pierre Indemini since our first meeting. One can be the unfeeling statue of an incredible emotion.

Already the crowded tables, the tuxedos, the women in leather, and about one hundred square feet with fifty dancers on top of each other had given me my habitual fright, and already I felt sick. But I had to. And the Englishman was there at the bar. All the fury of that evening's fun was concentrated in that libidinous man or animal. In love with anyone at all, man or woman, his head thrown back in ecstasy, he was vibrating in time with the jazz and his hands moving back and forth in front of him were tracing his dreams: a gang of yapping Americans. And now I go up to the Englishman, I take his hand, I propose that we dance. He looks at me, this misshapen dancing girl, and off we go. Hup! I had had the time to shout to Pierre Indemini, "There's a vacant table in the back to the left!"

I felt the drunken Englishman against me.

When at last I went back to *him,* I had only one thought in my mind—how did that happen, how was the Englishman able to gain such power over me? But I had another crazy impulse. I put my elbows on the table and I sang.

During the break, an English jingle came out of my lips (it has to be spoken in the most French-sounding English possible):

Oh which do you like to see, M'sieu
Oh which do you like to see:
That haughty, proud American Girl
Or the lady from Gay Paree—
Oh the gay Pari-si-enne,
She do capture all the men
With the naughty little way
She has of
        M—m—
                Walking . . .

And then I lay my head on my arms, and

Oh which do you like to see, M'sieu
Oh which do you like to see . . .

I burst into tears.

Could *he* love a girl like me? Everything, everything, always, said no. "Would such a girl dare to lift her eyes again in his presence? As far back as I can remember, the thing that was meant for me and that I cherished the most, I would deliberately make that thing fail. My first sin, that cloud over everything, the sin of existing, which has never been pardoned, do you understand, are you going to understand? How would you understand, since you don't know me. And so this is what I imagined to make myself known, and it is *not even true!* I want to call you to me: Oh Stranger . . . That you but understand. That you but understand. So that you say to me—"

His hand slipped a silk handkerchief under my face, and he seemed to me as merciful as a saint when he said softly, "Would you like to take my arm and go out, Catherine? I understand perfectly what has happened to you."

Yet people were whispering my name: "Catharina . . . It's Catharina . . . " I preferred to raise my head.

I began, "Now tell me what you are."

I ordered something to drink. The jazz tune they were playing was heartrending. He was not frightened and answered me, "Your eyes are shining with a painful brightness. Do you have a fever?"

He insisted that I let him take me home.

"No, right here, tell your story."

He had called me "Catherine." Against my chest I felt his first letter. So everything was not lost. Jack's awfulness slid off him and left him unimpaired. How was I supposed to look at him? With my face very close to his, to blot out, to drive away horrible enemy forms? How was I supposed to look at him? Because more and more he seemed devoted to me, and with very simple phrases he told me what I wanted to know.

His father was from the Val d'Aosta and had grown up there. That was why his name was Italian! He himself had been born in Paris. And I was born in Savoy, I told him. There was only a mountain range between us. He had only one relative left in the country, who was looking after his property, but he was going to sell everything. As for me, I have always been an orphan and poor. His age: almost twenty-five. My God! I was over twenty-six! And tears overcame me again.

I have only to close my eyes—and Pierre Indemini's smile comes back to me from times past. Oh Pierre's smile! Blessed be thou, first smile at Jack's. Despite me and despite him and despite everything, and despite what happened, afterward.

I told him I was a movie actress. Because I was imploring his mercy now. I felt that he didn't like that for me. He had never seen me on-screen.

Anyway, he was not mistaken about my heart, in spite of that awful Jack's place.

"And you, what do you do?"

"What I do is just as surprising as your movies."

"Well, what is it?"

"I'm involved in the philosophy of mathematics."

I said to him, "Is that all?"

He must have taken me for an idiot, and without any doubt I deserved it. I was unhappy. I turned in another direction: "Do you have a mistress?"

"No."

This time I burst out laughing and pulled him outside.

V

I needed to stare at him for a long time, stare at him and study him. This was what I did during the middle of the night. Then I kissed his letter in front of him as a sign of complete acceptance and I begged him to leave me; without anything having happened.

It's always enough to say yes . . . to say no . . .

The next day, the same night, the same scene. He was in no more of a hurry than I to arrive at that.

My joy was profound. Pierre Indemini loved me for myself. At the same time, curious reversals, it was I who loved at last and it was my own being that I adored. I, the sad face, immediately alarmed everybody with "my ferocious appetite," my gaiety, and my magnificent ideas. But, before that, I must tell the story of the blue line. From twenty to perhaps twenty-three, I had observed a secret ritual. It was *the blue line* and it consoled me oddly for my solitude. On my body, after my bath, I would draw a wavy blue line with makeup down the middle of my chest. When night came and I saw the blue line again (always as though I had for-gotten it), I would feel a childish joy, clap my hands. Or would I give way to some fond meditation on myself? Immediately after the evening at Jack's I began the blue line again, with the feeling that my ritual had now taken on a beauty that nothing could have given it before. The happiness I derived from it was so intense that I above all did not want to tamper, through an act with Pierre Indemini, with my love secrets, thus brought together. I lived in fantasy: the line and Pierre were the dreams of my own beauty, with strange echoes, bits of music snatched from the air which arose deep within my ears. Oh, how wonderful it was: he knew nothing of all this. I said many tender things to him, and not those of the true depths. I was in love, a liar. Oh, how I desired that all this should continue thus suspended! And that it should never be *done* in order to remain (extraordinary in price and in beauty . . .).

However, we are weak and the loveliest moments tremble. . . . After three weeks of this reserved paradise I felt sure of myself and of him. One night I leaned toward him because we were reading together. In a rush of warmth I wanted to imitate what we were reading. And so I leaned toward him. I saw him redden, grow younger, and saw his face approach the opening of my blouse. (He had never permitted himself to direct his gaze to it.) (I understood afterward.) He had noticed the blue line. He fol-lowed the blue line toward the deepest part of me. Then imme-diately I let myself be taken by him. All force gone.

And do you know that, as the joy became real, earthly, of the flesh, and as the love was expressed, there was nothing different?

In the room above the dark garden. Love is a bird that flies in and flies out. Love is a blade of grass that we feel at night and in the daytime just as well. About love we no longer know any-thing, since we have it. It is a strange sigh somewhere. We make love, therefore we try to capture it, but our happiness is already complete. It escapes us and we are without direction. Pierre's head on my breast.

VI

There is nothing to say about love except that it lasts, and first of all that it is, that one feels that it is, whereas one had sworn it would never be! That it is with a heat under one's eyes, a trembling in one's hands, that it is a sort of coloration of one's life and of all objects, a coloration so beautiful and so heartbreaking that it does not have the right to fade a thousandth of a degree, because then one would immediately fear that it was dying. One also feels that this holy coloration is under a perpetual threat, has nothing certain, for it always depends on interpretation: he is such as he is for me, I such as I am for him, and in the end the torment, and the force of the desire, come from what one desires within oneself but *in the other.* This is why one is so afraid and why love makes every effort to resemble a fireworks display.

Like every woman who is loved, I clearly sensed that this Desire and the submission it demands were the true end toward which, like a stream, I had flowed without knowing it. Had I been alive earlier, during my revolt when I fought in every way not to be a woman? No, I answered, no; now I will obey. And yet what I was discovering was not "love," it was *Pierre.* An obscure enchantment comes out of the underground passages of the heart and overflows, it is inevitable, necessary, but you are not explaining the secret of the enchantment: *Pierre for Catherine, Catherine for Pierre, him, her,* and not two others in all of eternity! Dazzled, overexcited, I worked the enchantment with all possible force. The enchantment will fail. . . . He and I—that is forever.

And so each of us lit the hidden fireworks and they formed a single burst of light. But we did not know each other. Much better, we did not want to know anything about each other. It was so beautiful the way it was. We wanted only to seize each other for a moment and immediately shout out victory.

I see his hair again, the hair of a young Venetian gentleman, his athletic shape, and his very white skin. He would say to me, "You're a nymph," and other times, "You're an angel," and finally "demon." As though with his words he were setting in motion a reality and we were going off enfolded within it. He would celebrate a part of my body that he would choose, with me absent, so to speak: my foot, my breast, my hip; and his dialogue with a part of me was so preposterous that I wished I were in his place in order to possess the secret of loving so madly. At last, after those ridiculous words "angel" and "nymph," which he had endowed with such great power (angel to me, Catherine Crachat, without a stitch, nymph to me, in my sad Paris apartment), and after the amorous litanies that I received like a statue, we would fall asleep, happy and fearful. He would spend the first part of the night with me. I had so young a sleep that I never knew when he left me.

And then, in that sort of shared life, I began to make him out, to know who he was. Reserved to an extreme and ill at ease in company, he suffered from being weak, by nature sad, and he would quickly become cruel enough to conceal it. His sensuality illuminated but frightened him. Without friends and enclosed in his strange work, he was ready for everything or nothing. An artist also, he wrote, and was contemptuous of being read and contemptuous of being known.

VII

Let us move ahead in time. A stone is lying on the road. A stone. This is a dream.

I am beginning to speak (with great difficulty, I assure you), to explain how I am moving my arm, that I am looking at it, all right, to give myself the proof, so that the sign (or the cygnet) that I have been may cease . . . and how the folded leg extends, extends and flattens out infinitely flat along the bed. All this multiplies rapidly and gives me proofs and allows me to lift myself up with the feeling that my back is an effort if not a real success. All of this does not stand out very clearly yet and rises again once or several times, and when the wall falls back again slantwise, the windowpane lets the moonlight through: then there is nothing to do, reality can no longer be attained, one must wait. Wait.

I am drawn from this diabolical enchantment by a sweet little memory of his shoulder with a patch of sweat on it, which I kiss, while his detachable collar is on the floor.

Everything changes. I see myself lying down—tired!—in my *young girl's bed*. A tree is growing from the mattress, between my knees and toward my hips, a hard tree, wicked as a crocodile. This tree condemns me to death; it causes me to be nailed alive into the earth. I am condemned to death but I'm not suffering. An old woman "who spent a long time in the theater" stands beside my bed and muses. She laughs from time to time. My blood is running out but the old woman is collecting it in her hands, saying, "We mustn't let it be lost." She adds that *at the end, fortunately,* they will hear me howl all over the world!

I woke up. I was in my bed and the face of the moon was looking at me. Early morning, one could hear the milkmen's trucks. Between Pierre's furtive and almost cowardly departure in the middle of the night . . . and this dream I had had afterward, I made an atrocious and monstrous connection.

I felt shame, fear. I realized I had no underwear next to my skin. I was overwhelmed with shame. I could not shake it off. Did I love him, yes or no? Did he love me, yes or no? Was loving different from making love?

I forgot the dream the next day; but the dream recurred—each time darker, more murderous, more distressing. I didn't talk about it to Pierre. I begged him to spend the whole night with me; he didn't consent.

Anguish had entered my house.

VIII

After this warning, in which I could make out nothing yet, I trembled with all my might. I had received a sign, perhaps from heaven, in any case having its source in our destiny. I trembled without showing him anything but a clear face, confident eyes, and I drove the trembling down inside my fear, so much so that after a little I was completely infected, but in order to save my love I played love as an actress. Even if he had figured me out, I could not have said anything to him about the nature of my suspicion: did I think love was forbidden, or our love impossible, or already over? At the same time I rooted Pierre in my heart as the real, the only plant of love in all my life. With him I wore the mask of confidence, false beauty . . . hypocritical gentleness . . . and I gave way to hours of tears when I was alone. I became absorbed in bizarre witchcraft to conjure fate, I was so convinced of the inevitable. He had to see my profile and never my face when he entered the bedroom, the opposite would have precipitated a catastrophe. I read auguries everywhere, in the slightest coincidences. I often refused to give in to his desire out of superstition with regard to desire, and I became very difficult. I redid my makeup twenty times during the day, and I worried about one mole on my skin, and I was terrible with everyone. I couldn't keep still out of agitation, and was always ready to break everything, bam!

Only Pierre Indemini, when he laid his hand over my eyes . . . Ten months of this kind of life (during which I acted in several big movies) formed my character.

And now, Catherine Crachat, back from London, was supposed to find Pierre Indemini at her friend Marguerite de Douxmaison's house.

Why this plan, which went against my instinct, to see my
lover again in the midst of all my friends? I've forgotten, if ever I
knew. We pretended to be as easy as husband and wife. I spent a
few hours sleeping at the rue Jacob and I arrived at Marguerite's.

Marguerite's pure, gray smile alone would guarantee that no
crime against me lies in the offing. I have a tender love for Marguerite. At the time she is forty-six years old, she is a widow, and
because she loves the art of film she receives our group on Tues-
days. She gives us her tenderness and a part of her fortune,
indeed we impose upon her rather a lot, but Marguerite de Douxmaison is so real, with so little worldliness and so little falseness
in her, perfect as her name—Sweet-house—indicates, that she
can always give without wasting her affections. She has *charity*—
which doesn't inhabit bodies like ours.

In fact, I was thinking while they were taking my coat from
me at the door, why wouldn't Pierre propose marriage to me? I
smiled at myself from head to toe in a mirror. My dress looked
very good on me. I was very striking. I was going to see Pierre
again. I went into the gallery of old paintings, busts, inhaling the
odor of marble, suddenly happy. I was taken into the orange living room, and Marguerite, seeing me from a distance, came up,
offered me her cheek; we embraced. Many well-known women,
few men—and no Pierre.

IX

Here is the event as it took place inside me. I'm recalling
everything.

Those women are there. Sitting. Standing. Specimens of large
made-up animals, each with its particular odor. I see teeth under

the chops. I detest them. I am one of them. I am very pleasant. Marguerite says to me with her glances: What's the matter, my little friend? You're pale. I answer her that, however kind she may be, the state of my heart is none of her business! She insists: He's not here yet but he will come, dove, he will! Don't worry. Are you afraid of something?

I am sitting next to Marguerite and I'm exchanging commonplace remarks with her about the trip I have just taken. I'm hot or cold. I realize that all the made-up animals who are my sisters are on one side and I am on the other. The great Cogan is asking in American if the Norwegian is comfortable. The great Cogan, the American who created hatless Madeleine in *Golgotha,* crosses her bronze legs above her knees, and her dress is slit under the arms, the first thing you see the buoyant thickness of her breast. Am I afraid! I'm afraid of the great Cogan; I'm afraid of Dolores, who is in black buttoned up to her neck, and it's as though she has just barely left the garbage vat in Tolstoy's *Resurrection;* I'm afraid of the two Migetts, those little Swiss girls who have no talent. I drink some port. I say what I like. The port goes to my head. I feel a conspiracy of glances and dresses against me. Marguerite is more uneasy. Enter a few men. A Prince Vassily introduces himself and heaps me with compliments, vast compliments, Russian-style, things vile enough to make you vomit. I turn my head. Now they're jealous, they're waiting. I stand up. The reason, the point, what? I don't know; they want to make me suffer. I accept it willingly. I take a few steps. I get rid of Vassily. Servandoni, that Roman slut, calls me by the hateful nickname "Ka-Ka," whose meaning is obvious; no one has dared to call me that for a long time.

"She got here in time."

Why in time? Cogan is the one talking, in French, but she's looking at me. Who is next to her? Pierre Indemini. Pierre Indemini is in a frock coat, extremely handsome and thoroughly distinguished. At that very moment my soul flutters violently about, like a caged bird, in a tumult, among those Parisian personages: this is what I would like to convey to you. *Yes, it is at this moment.*

Pierre Indemini, after greeting Marguerite, greets me; he kisses my hand.

I understand everything clearly. Pierre Indemini is next to Cogan again. Next to her buoyant breast. The buoyant breast is heaving. Cogan is as strong as a prairie. I move a little farther away still. Marguerite tries to distract me. I resist. No! I must verify it meticulously. Mind you, I know very well that he doesn't give a damn about Cogan, and she, that great imbecile of a prairie, doesn't know she's being made a fool of. But Pierre and I are engaged in a duel.

I am patient, I bite my lip and neaten my hair with my finger. Obviously, if I had a little presence of mind I could restore everything, if there was a little strength still at liberty in my heart. I can walk up to Pierre casually. I can take him away on my arm. He belongs to me. I have the right to demand a properly executed severance, but at my place.

He had turned back into what he had first seemed, the man I knew that evening at Jack's, kind, excited, a little affected, and very young. Younger than he had been with me during the year that had just gone by, more abandoned to himself. More full of promise. Fresher. He had the lightness of a *stranger*. He seemed as free as the air.

It wasn't jealousy that made me draw a breath and form a resolution, it wasn't rage or sadness. No. I am suppressing my sight, I have no more sensations of light. I am suppressing my hearing, no one is talking around me now, there is silence. I still have my body a little and I can feel my limbs; then I don't feel them anymore. I am bent toward the inside, toward myself; I feel, as I have never felt before, that I am a thought, and I let something rise up, only something that wants to rise up, that wants to be. I feel it fly, here, there, in the darkness, and then I feel that it has come and that now I must let it be done.

At last I stand up very slowly, I recover the use of the living room and I go forward. I am close to them. Cogan points her headlights at me; Pierre's youth disappears. I pass by them slowly, very heavily, and I open my mouth and I say, clearly enough for Pierre alone to hear, but also Cogan if she wants and even the people around: "Good-bye Pierre. You're free."

Pierre Indemini receives it, there is a brief struggle, and then he yields. Cogan is distressed, but naturally she laughs, naturally. I pass by.

"You're free."

I pass by. Completely and forever, this time.

In the gallery, I gestured to Marguerite, who was bewildered, that I did not want any *speeches*. Like Rachel, she does not consent to be consoled. I accepted a glass of water. I threw myself into my car, then into my bed. For days and days I had a hellfire in my head and did not sleep, but he did not appear there and I worked as usual. One would think that a disease of the body, an infection with pain, would respond to the collapse of the living part of your soul. It isn't true at all. One walks on, annihilated. One is quite alive, one's life destroyed. This is the letter from Pierre Indemini that I read two days later: "I would not have dared suggest to you such a harsh separation, Catherine, it is you who impose it by taking pains to humiliate me. The reason why you acted would be laughable if it were not so fundamental. But it is fundamental. You are a lunatic lover, and a cruel one. Know in any case that I leave you Mademoiselle Cogan. Good-bye. Pierre."

Catherine had thrust her hand into her shirt and removed two letters tied together, and read the one about the breakup, and shown the other and both together:

"This letter, too, I put against my breast. You see. With the first. I still have it."

CATHERINE MEETS FANNY FELICITAS

X

The home of a certain dancer around 1820 or 1830, a friend of Schubert's or some such story, is located in a steeply descending lane, in Heiligenstadt. This is one of the "preserved bits" of a city that has a large number of them. The dancer is not extraordinarily important, she shone brightly and faded; but since her death, thanks to the meticulously preservationist spirit of the city of Vienna, as light as a poetic symbol, her presence signaled by a marble plaque, she still reverberates in the peaceful neighborhood of Heiligenstadt. But she is equally associated with the shadow of the irascible Beethoven, which dominates this little country. Even though one can now see the chimneys of Floridsdorf and the factory districts of the Danube from the dancer's attic, one feels one is situated exclusively, when one enters the dancer's two rooms, in the milieu of musical loves that are a hundred years old, and one is visited by a pleasant "sentiment" that extends from these loves, from these old tutus, to us and our modern preoccupations, and for instance includes in its attractive ramifications the figure of this tall young woman, with her slightly mechanical elegance, beautiful, with a boyish look, who is answering letters on a typewriter. She's the tenant of the place. She arrived a week ago, and she feels so good here that she dreams of winding the thread of her entire life on this spool. Alas, she has taken the place for only a month.

As the traveler interrupts herself in order to have a look at her two rooms, let us look with her. Clearly, this is the dancer's dressing room, which has been transported to a country spot. Same red-pink and rice-powder atmosphere. The tone of the walls is supposed to bring out the softness of the skin, the line of the shoulders, the shimmering satin. It is so small that it couldn't pass for a house. The antechamber, where one can't take more than two steps, contains a couch and portraits; a door colored with pinks of an acid tone opens flush with the ceiling and scrapes when opened; and here is the room where one sleeps very well in a pleasant yellow Biedermeier-period cradle, above which a mirror leans widthwise (it's for seeing oneself).

After which the young woman's glances pass through the little window that is absurd or touching, whichever you like, and roam outside. It is right in the middle of June, the weather now is very beautiful. When, through this window, one remembers Paris, the contrast is so violent that one could allow one's heart to break.

XI

Mademoiselle C. cut short the demonstrations of her invisible self, so inclined to recollection, whose needs are so "poetic"; she shrugged her shoulders and pushed the typewriter off into a corner, gathered up the letters, wrote the addresses on them, put the stamps on them, stood up, smoothed her hair with her hand, knocked against the table. Let the dead bury the dead.

Since the second episode was being performed at the château at two o'clock, she had an hour and forty-five minutes to get into town and have lunch, which was perfectly convenient.

A tap-tap was heard.

The good Madame Schramek, in other words, the landlady, made a discreet appearance on the lower steps of the stairway, rapping the wall with her dry finger, which the years had made rather like the woodwork.

In her bad French, full of nuances and employing much refinement, Madame Schramek explained that a *visit* was there: a lady of society, accompanied by her son, requested the honor of being admitted to Mademoiselle.

Can one resist Madame Schramek? For the young tenant, this endearing old person was the source of a feeling of—how shall one put it—confidence, as though in the last week Madame

Schramek had done more for her than anyone else in the world. Traveling inclines one to such sweet illusions.

The two women hadn't even "talked about a serious matter"; but as the foreigner had in her luggage some rather heavy sorrows, Madame Schramek had seen them and sheltered them with a particular zeal. Nothing but petty details of practical life, between Madame Schramek and her tenant, like the place of the new candle and the matches at nighttime by the front entrance; the coffee and milk in the morning followed by hot water; at what time the one and what time the other; the clothes dried after a rainy evening; the room tidied up and "everything you like" arranged "as you would wish." Such was the symbolic language used by Madame Schramek to make her way toward the more serious subjects. She carried in her hand, in order to transmit it to you, a marvelous light that she must have found when she was young in the distant isles or in dreams, and which since then she had been expending very prudently, without waste or greed.

"Here is Madame Schramek bringing me one of her old friends . . . Well of course, let her come in, Madame Schramek."

A rather stout lady appeared, pink and vivacious, dressed with negligent care; she held out an enormous sheaf of garnet-red roses. Madame Schramek clasped her hands together in contentment and disappeared.

"Oh, what roses!" the foreigner exclaimed spontaneously.

The lady answered: "*We're neighbors,* Mademoiselle Catharina. I found out only yesterday and I was so delighted" (the lady spoke a clear and transparent French, with a few awkwardnesses) "that it was no longer possible for me to stay *in my corner!* Nor to keep my roses for myself, thinking that you were so close and that these roses which made me so happy did not exist for you! Baroness Fanny Felicitas Hohenstein."

"I'm pleased to know you," said Catherine, automatically but with a certain artistry. She held out her hand, which was clasped by the Baroness Hohenstein with mute feeling.

"But so many roses. . . . Are they really for me?"

"What a nice little house you have found! Wasn't Clara Wende's home just made for you? How very pretty it is." (The lady looked around and smiled a very beautiful smile, warm and deep, which showed her bluish teeth.) "When I was informed of your trip to Vienna, Mademoiselle Catharina, it was done, you were already among us. And so I was not able to suggest that you stay in my home—for such was my very great desire! I have admired you for many years, and I will dare to say also that I am a little in love with you. I was truly saddened; and when I found out yesterday that you were in Clara Wende's house, I realized that I was wrong to want you in my house, but I couldn't restrain myself from coming to see you."

The roses were laid on the table.

"Are they really for me?" Catherine reiterated, becoming immersed little by little in a painful dream, her question out of place.

"*For you.*"

"You are too generous."

"My garden is too generous; but you—you are admirable."

"Oh no. So we are neighbors?"

"I live in 'Ruh-Land,' which is between here and Grinzing, ten minutes away. I hope you will be so kind as to come see me? My roses are demanding it of you."

"But of course I will come . . . "

Catherine was already calculating the difficulties of the social relations and was frightened.

"When?" said the Baroness Hohenstein gently.

"Forgive me, I have so much work . . . "

"Oh yes, it's so wonderful! I'm told that you are performing at the Château de Schoenbrunn. And what about the evening?"

"In the evening I sleep."

"Your answer is wonderful too. But for *me* one evening?"

All of a sudden she is perfectly wonderful (she too), winning, without powder or rouge on her face, natural, the most charming woman of the Viennese or Bavarian type; and she seems unpretentious.

"I'm a recluse," Catherine confesses.

"You will see my husband, who admires you as much as I do, and my big son. That's all."

"Your son . . . Wasn't he with you?"

"He is waiting for me downstairs in the courtyard."

Baroness Hohenstein goes on, "The day after tomorrow?"

Catherine answers almost joyously, "The day after tomorrow."

The visitor, bowing her neck in her shirt collar, resumes the questioning air she had at the beginning of the meeting, and a cloud passes over her: "What favor you have received from heaven, to be what you are! In you, life is true, real, whereas in me . . . But anyway, my son will come to fetch you."

XII

Inexplicable correspondences: after this baroness left, five years of being Catherine Crachat appeared before her, years that demanded to be judged. They had to be appreciated in detail and collectively in their *negative* value as a sad symptom of the malady of her life. Through an effect of contrast, Catherine's eyes traversed the city, extremely gay under the new heat of summer, and saw the cafés, the flowers, and the human figures, the gleaming rails of the red tramways, and very tall, very green trees in whose shadow walked handsome boys and robust girls, singing.

Five years (since the breakup at Marguerite de Douxmaison's house) sprang unexpectedly from the Baroness Hohenstein's roses. Catherine in Vienna was no longer in Vienna but in herself for five years, in the rue Jacob. She wasn't crying on a sofa, no, more likely she was slamming doors, coming in and going out. She would change her dress ten thousand times. Five nothing, empty, nasty years, with "heaps" of money and bags of candies and lots of chocolate and on her body every possible expensive thing. Five years for nothing, "in which I didn't even suffer what I should have." Luxury and notoriety, and, underneath, one lone, one single misfortune in love large enough to blow the props out from under the whole of life. She asked it aloud, shaking her head: how was I able?

. . . Strange name: Fanny Felicitas. Curious woman. Too beautiful roses. As she interrupted the general din with her own din and let her thoughts float with the motion of the open car, Catherine was saying: And when will I ever be able to defend myself? Just because this baroness admires me, did I have to open the door to her? Thanks to her I have already had an attack of *remembering;* tomorrow I'll be in the dumps, the day after I'll lapse back into my *sins.* Because this misery, these sins, revive as soon as anyone, no matter who, looks at me a little tenderly. Then Catherine saw before her again: Pierre. "One would do much better to kill *him,*" she said out loud. The driver turned around; he understood French. Catherine burst out laughing.

Was it the laughter, the roses, what? But the worthless and shameful time she had lived through after losing that man Pierre Indemini appeared on top of another memory; suddenly she could see that her suffering had changed, this very morning: it was distant, cooler, and most importantly no longer inside her but in front of her. As though these private beasts that make us perform so many frightful moves and commit base acts in order to "forget" or to "get him back again," once they were brought into the light of this Vienna morning, under a superb sky, in an atmosphere of hope, turned out quite evidently to be dead after all; and as though the rage had passed outside, now tranquil, belonging to the world, sadness, smiling . . . Catherine would now have to carry within her only a thing that was defunct, true, but that had been lived through and was finally *accepted.*

All of this, so new, began with some roses . . . The roses of the Baroness Hohenstein.

XIII

On the Opera Ring, her car passed the two Migetts.

"Catharina! Stop." The car took them on board.

"Hello, Migetts." One needed to say only a single hello for the two of them.

"Hello, Catherine, how are you?"

The Migetts were very much in form this morning, perfect. The Migetts are the same, as identical as two replicas of one pretty and disturbing statuette. They have in common: their age (they are twins); their black eyes; their curled eyelashes; their curly brown hair; their noses, with cruel little nostrils; their porcelain look; their voices (easily mistaken for each other); their willowy figures and no breasts; lastly, their dresses.

Except that one is in blue and the other in green; the one in blue is Flore. What this is is the same *girl* repeated twice by Mother Nature. Even if one is used to it, as Catherine is, it's always very amusing. The Migetts, little girls from the Swiss Jura (their name is Miget) became acquainted with the glory of the boulevards at age sixteen, but their conduct is moral. They are the *co-optimists* of the group. They are thought to be virgins. Is it useful to point out that they began acting and dancing with the help of the organizations of the M.G.A. (abbreviation for "Music-hall and Cinema Girls Association") in London and Paris, run by the pastors and offering "hundreds of nice-looking poor girls a place of refuge and moral support outside their working hours"?

Catherine, however, is skeptical. And in fact Migett says, "We're going out tonight. Can you come too, Catharina?"

"Where?"

"We're going to the opera with Pastor Tweedmann. Before that we're having dinner at Pastor Tweedmann's house. And then we're going to bed, but at midnight could we have supper together?"

"With Pastor Tweedmann?"

"No, no, without him!"

It's funny, this morning they look to Catherine like a married couple together.

"Who is this pastor?"

"The M.G.A.'s agent in Vienna. He's an old, rather batty Englishman. He's in love with Flore!"

"No, with Céline!"

"With you."

"With you."

Their cascading laughter refreshed Catherine's heart, and the driver turned around once again, "at the risk getting us all banged up in an accident."

During lunch, Migett turns serious.

"My dears, I love Vienna. It's pretty and it's wealthy. People have told me about a lady who belongs to the best society. True, she's apparently perhaps just a little Jewish, but one never knows, and she married a Catholic baron, a journalist. The lady is a Catholic baroness. Or countess. It doesn't matter. Not too pretty, you might say, but she has always had heaps of men and women at her heels. One of her lovers apparently committed suicide— really did. That made quite a stir. She also has a collection of pictures. She's head of a women's beauty society that consists of being naked in gardens."

"You're exaggerating," says Catherine.

"Not one bit. It's all true. The best part is the last: the lady adores the movies, and she adores all of us. Not the men, only the women stars. I tell you she's crazy with admiration. She wants to gather the whole cast of *The Beggar Girl* in her home . . . "

The Beggar Girl, Catherine, is reminded of her tragedy again.

HEROINE IN A GREAT NATION'S FIGHT FOR INDEPENDENCE, LOLA, DISGUISED AS A BEGGAR, SLIPS INTO THE COURT, APPROACHES THE EMPEROR OF AUSTRIA . . .

The second subtitle to be created that afternoon. Accoutrement. Wall to the left. Oblique movement . . .

" . . . and I have a wonderful time whenever I go there. But do you know who she is looking for, who she wants more than anyone else, who she is courting? Who? Who? Catharina."

"Of course!" said Catherine irritably.

"Oh, how funny you are! The way you say that . . . I tell you . . . " Céline Migett is feeling very annoyed now.

Flore, who knows what's coming, shrugs her shoulders.

But Catherine is thinking about the roses again. These Viennese women are a nuisance. The one Migett is talking about must be the one who wrote to me, Countess Schel . . . I don't remember anymore.

When their car let them off in front of the château, Migett leaped out first, crying: "The magnificent Catharina! The magnificent Catharina!" so that Catherine had to tap her on the calves with her little cane to make her be quiet.

XIV

The Baroness Hohenstein's home was a museum. Before a somber, lofty, brilliant, and sumptuous reality, with lines contorted by pride or faith, Catherine halted in suspense.

The baroness made it clear that this museum was her personal creation; the work of selecting and buying, and then of displaying the rarest old examples of a certain genre that interested her, had taken her many years.

Fanny Felicitas's rooms would delight whatever soul was brought into them, even the most pragmatic and bourgeois; but anyone prevailed upon to stay there, to live there, to feel at home there, and amidst so much magnificence to chat in a natural voice with the mistress of the house, was obliged to make a certain effort of adaptation, to adopt a certain attitude.

"These are mainly 'high Baroque' pieces because I was crazy about that at one time," explains Fanny Felicitas in a tone of joyous humility.

The house was very brightly lit. Objects polished by the ages gleamed and shone. Baroness Fanny was not afraid of quantity, but never spoiled anything by clutter. Among these materials and these forms on which time was so gloriously inscribed, each piece of furniture or rug or chandelier or enamel being a choice and splendid specimen that had weathered several selections within the type to which it belonged, among so many things which one's gaze immediately praised lavishly, space itself acquired a force and a softness, the quality of a masterpiece.

Surrounded by this imperious beauty, the Baroness Fanny, having taken a moment before appearing herself, seemed to apologize:

"Excuse me," she said, "but I could not make my decor disappear with a wave of the magic wand."

"And why make it disappear?"

"It bothers me. *For you* I would like a more intimate place, and a livelier one."

It often happened, the baroness said, that a visitor, having made the initial efforts, having then evinced a large measure of emotion and admiration, would seem to tire, to sink into hesitancy, and from hesitancy into ill humor. Fanny Felicitas was accustomed to it. It is even imaginable that she took a certain pleasure in experiencing the lassitude or incomprehension of an "intelligent" person. "In the midst of all this," she said, "I myself am the spider."

Everywhere she turned, Catherine read, painted on wood or glass, engraved or cast, in gold, in marble, embroidered, the holy monogram

I H S

evidence of ancient ecclesiastical ostentation, and Catherine felt a secret uneasiness which she was constrained to keep to herself; for support Catherine looked to the person of the seductive "spider." Who are you? What reason do you have for accumulating these objects which for you do not count? What sort of woman was this?

"To think that you are sitting in my house, Mademoiselle Catharina!"

"As you see. Does it seem so extraordinary to you?"

"Oh, you have not been spoiled by your fame. For you it's nothing, is it? I am *in heaven*," Madame Hohenstein said again.

Her rather plump form with a lower lip describing a slight pout; dimples, magnificent teeth. Her eyes are pale and resemble the sheets of water on mountains on a windy day: a profound light blue. Solid body, probably muscular, as bodies were in antiquity. This fighter with the soft shapes is wearing a peasant dress, from the Tyrol, gray with festoons of blue wool.

"This house, or nothing at all—it comes to the same, doesn't it? Say it, I want to hear it from you. I would love it if you were the one to say it."

"No, not at all, the house is very beautiful, you are an artist."

"Don't mock me, don't make fun of me! If only you knew the distress"—tears in her eyes—"that lies beneath these beautiful objects."

Catherine maintains a prudent (abominable) silence.

"It is so sad to be a Felicitas."

"Why do you belittle yourself?" Catherine threw out.

"But *you,* to be *you,* to have your talent, your beauty, your charm; oh, my God!"

After a while Felicitas went on: "Oh, I'm not belittling myself. It's more complicated for me than you can believe. I like myself very much. One always likes oneself very much, isn't that so?"

"Very much."

"You like yourself, really? You feel it?"

"I am not answering your question, it's too direct," said Catherine with simplicity.

"I like myself and detest myself in the same breath, and one as strongly as the other." Baroness Hohenstein pressed a thin ivory button scarcely visible in the plaster wall. "You will take a cup of tea? . . . But first I would have to know *who* I am. I've asked many individuals, and no one has answered me. No, no one. Now tell me what you think of me, for instance: am I a rich and intriguing woman?"

"Why, I don't think anything about you! Not yet." And Catherine began to laugh. "I find you very congenial."

"Oh Mademoiselle Catharina! You don't know what I expect from you. Anyway, forgive me for flinging myself at your head in my joy at having you with me. Now I will be completely reasonable."

Tea was served by a meticulous maid and Catherine was given a cup. The tea was wonderful.

"In France you say sympathetic and interesting. A picture is interesting. A woman is *sympathique.* I don't like that. This alone I did not like in Paris, for Paris I love, but this politeness and this intelligence in the place of sentiment, and the coldness—you say coldness?"

"Coldness, yes, but I am not cold!"

"How nice it is, I feel that we are going to understand each other. You are Catharina, you are a sister for me. I have loved you for ten years because I have seen you in *all your roles.* In *Elegy—*

Spilled Blood—The Little Girl—and also *The Outcast of the Islands:* magnificent! What reality, what power, what fascination. You have expressed today's woman, untamable and broken, who has caused her chains to fall and who seeks, and cannot find in herself, the male force of power!"

"I hate the cinema," Catherine said rather sharply. "It's my profession."

"How I like you. There is nothing greater than rejecting what one is."

"You," said Catherine, "I like you too—more and more, I have to confess."

XV

And so Catherine was sitting in light diffused by a large lampshade made of eighteenth-century Chinese silk fabric in the corner of a vast, dark room. With the objects asleep, everything became calm. A sense of fine quality emanated from the small smiling baroness. The *Gemüt* of Vienna was at its highest degree, for it melted in the air leaving only traces. That evening Catherine was wearing a silk blouse with a single small black knot next to the collar, her hair, not clinging to her head, in a cloud, her face powdered and her mouth barely enlarged. They looked at each other. They breathed distant things, indefinable. They felt they were in Austria. They felt very good.

She is good, Catherine imagined; she must be good. Personal, obviously; but her manners are noticeably and charmingly natural, not at all severe or elegant. There are no rings on her fingers. Her face is without affectation. She presents it with ardor, and directly. She is always ingenuous and "dimpling," like the young girl she used to be when she was waiting for a fiancé. Her freshness is astonishing.

Rest. Think. Look at me.

At that point the door opened, a door ornamented like a house, dating from 1750; and in the opening Catherine saw two men.

One rather short and corpulent (the husband); one would have said his face had a natural glumness, and yet he seemed to be extremely pleasant. That contradiction could be seen even in the shape of his head, which was flat, bare on top and behind, with an expressive forehead hiding two intelligent eyes. The other personage exceeded in height everyone and everything, being topped only by the most monumental of the armoires. He was smiling. He was frankly fat, but that was almost unnoticeable, he stepped sideways for fear he would break the furniture.

"My husband. My son."

At the words "my son," Baroness Fanny's voice weakened slightly and slowed.

The two very stiff men bent down before Catherine, took her hand, and kissed it one after the other in exactly the same spot.

This extraordinary son who was afraid to take a seat wore leather breeches wrinkled across the lower abdomen, a short jacket of blue linen, an embroidered shirt, and his neck and knees were bare. Such a costume at ten o'clock at night no longer surprised Catherine, but she looked especially at the son, whose face was handsome and simple like a slice of white bread.

Baron Siegmund Hohenstein began speaking and one had to answer him. The conversation about film became general.

XVI

Siegmund Hohenstein was the editor of Vienna's foremost reactionary newspaper. That is to say, he was in a good position to welcome a famous French actress into his drawing room on special terms. In connection with this, he showed an interest, into which several different ingredients entered, in Catherine's native country. He pointed out that his paper had previously had occasion to express, before the other organs of the Viennese press had done so, the admiration people felt here for Catharina's principal creations—and Baron Hohenstein swaggered slightly and stopped, then quite quickly released the brakes in order to be able to continue. Catherine pretended to remember several reviews in the *Neue Zeitung* (but remembered nothing at all).

This baron, apparently a good man, manifested a certain distance in his tone. Was it class prejudice? Or a susceptibility to national feeling? Or rather an inclination, capable of becoming keen, for Catherine's physical person? All three.

The diplomacy of a first reception at the Villa Ruh-Land did not prevent one from perceiving in the Baron Hohenstein a sadness and a hollowness; it was sometimes as though with the contractions of his face he seemed to be calling for help. Suddenly Catherine thought back to Céline Migett's piece of gossip, identified the Viennese lady as this one here, recalled the stories— and regarded Fanny Felicitas with a fresh eye.

In the days that followed, the family picture developed before Catherine in the following manner.

M. Hohenstein exchanged nothing with his wife. They kept silent; they were very courteous toward each other. The baron and the son had affectionate, comradely relations, and it was clear "that this was not his son." The son manifested toward his parents a great, if slightly mocking, respect, but a respect that attached profoundly to every least reality emanating from his mother. The baron, when referring to them together, said by way of a joke, "Him and Her," and underscored this joke with a grin. All of Fanny's affectivity, except for the part that was directed toward Catharina, rested upon *the son,* had him for its base, but in an unstable manner, like a pyramid balanced on its tip.

His name is Guido. He is not the child of Baron Hohenstein, he is the son of Fanny's first husband. Guido makes a distinction between "my father" and "my real father." To judge from certain allusions, it seems that the real father is in Vienna.

Fanny Felicitas played with this young colossus the game of having brought him into the world. A complicated game, full of subtle events, full of manners, which led her to appear, for her part, a very young girl. On the other hand, Baron Hohenstein openly poked fun at Guido for being indifferent to women (looking at the beautiful Catherine, for instance, as though she were a horse). Fanny, probably having the key to Guido's situation, was indulgent; more than indulgent, protective.

Baron Siegmund retired fairly early, shortly followed by the son. Baroness Fanny Felicitas turned off the lamps that were not needed and the two of them remained alone together under the Chinese lampshade.

Her eyes took on a bright gleam between her chestnut lashes. Faint circles surrounded them tenderly. A woman who has just passed her fortieth year, in the fullness of her life. A woman who loves passionately what she seeks, what she loves, what is going to love her; who excludes no object from her love. Who feels everything, who wants everything, who has no repose; who is formed anew like the phoenix in loving. And transfigured she looks at Catherine. The moment before she was alluding to long suffering between Herr Hohenstein and herself. Now she says to Catherine, "I love you," so kindly that Catherine does not blush and does not dream of taking offense.

XVII

. . . They had been welcoming, sensitive, and warm. Catherine was leaving Vienna.

She felt she had not traveled for nothing. At Ruh-Land she had left behind some friends. Leaving. Always leaving. Go away and come back? Always meeting up with herself again at the street corner. She had left the home of the dancer, Madame Schramek, and the cradle bed, just this morning: that, at least, was certainly over. She had hardly had a chance to enjoy it, "out all the time." Her mornings there, the lilac sky a little heavy, and the girls with young breasts, walking gaily on the raised earthen sidewalks that overlook the street between the properties . . . The night before, one last visit to Baroness Fanny had shown her pathetic people, preoccupied with the problems of their life, and so on. And she had promised to "come back." And now here she is with her suitcases at her feet in the West Bahnhof, waiting to go to the platform and board the Paris sleeping car. Does this mean life is only a matter of the calendar? She concluded: I was taken with Vienna. I loved the electric lights under the linden trees. Anyway, the movie will be a failure. Will I see the Hohensteins again? And I didn't really understand, in the end, what was going on at Ruh-Land.

To distract you, here's some news from your home: read this letter from Pola Servandoni while the train goes on its way.

"My dearest I don't have a sou. I'm not filming and I'm at Charenton with friends. I really envy you for working in foreign cities.

"Here it is neither pretty nor ugly. We have the illusion we're out in the country. We're not far from the Seine, but it's a spot where people who are fed up with life choose to throw themselves into the water. Since I've been here, there have been three already. The third was fished out just in time, but when she was revived, she started shouting, 'Let me die!' up and down the river. One really felt it would have been better to let her do it. As for the second, the rescue committee for the drowned searched for her for three days, but since these gentlemen only work from ten to five and then go off, they haven't found her. The little woman at the lock, who is like a little rose, said to me: 'Don't worry, they'll find her in the dam, they all end up getting caught in it.'

" . . . Catha, my dear, this is a rather macabre letter. Don't let it make you sad, though, I'm full of energy."

Paris! It's Paris.

Here's the rue Jacob again, the light gray weather, the noise, the immense humanity, neutral and deceptive. This Paris life which from afar seems impossible, which one reenters so easily.

XVIII

That summer it rained a great deal. It rained on the rue Jacob, and she put her face to the wet panes of the windows overlooking the garden.

Vienna is far away. Those flowers I gazed at, those bouquets of roses in a line at the tops of their stalks at dusk no longer exist at all. Those people so full of charm—I never knew them.

Vienna softened me all over. Have I such a need to be cherished? That trip oddly made me to turn to myself and find myself again after having lost myself.

But I am not going to take it any farther, I am not going to turn all this to account and maintain a friendship with Felicitas. Every human relationship and every pleasant anecdote, in my life, is destined to perish.

Baroness Hohenstein sends me complicated letters whose French makes me laugh. I have no indulgence and no desire to understand, I find nothing to answer.

I am incapable of preserving a love. Life changes and I am incapable of changing with it. What if I were to return to Ruh-Land? But to do what? Isn't it obvious that I am a failure in every posture I assume? Or another explanation comes to mind, which is that I always betray myself on purpose.

But what if I were to return to Vienna?

She was bored to death. She was in pitch darkness. Should she go on like this? How was she to stop this useless destruction?

Look, she said to her portrait in the mirror, look at Catherine Crachat. Me. Me whom I have loved so much. Me who disgusts me, annoys me, sets my nerves on edge. It is impossible that this woman should be me. *This woman doesn't have an honest look.*

Pierre Indemini still skimmed past the walls, an irresolute ghost. Always that one. But he is inseparable from the rue Jacob.

Another day that same summer (decidedly a black one) she saw light in the case of Pierre Indemini.

Pierre Indemini = cowardly nature. The mind is rich, the heart friable. Everything is promised and nothing will be kept: for this man flees from himself. One sees enough of them nowadays, these dazzling young men; they have square shoulders and are like empty suitcases. Perhaps they are desperate. They hurl themselves in every direction, they will have all sorts of energy, all sorts of courage, nothing will daunt them. Yet, simply enough, they have been *afraid,* they have been so awfully afraid at the outset . . . These men are the latest model, all steel. But the steel has a flaw: the boy lies down and begins crying. To begin with, they have trouble controlling a woman and this is what makes them cruel. They don't love anything. They no longer give anything. Oh, deceivers! They are handsome, like Indemini. At first I thought he contained an angel. Alas, what an angel! It was a failure. How can one suffer one's love pain for so long without wanting to understand the person? Because I don't mean one would have loved him any less, I mean that one would have delivered oneself from him, after the betrayal, by one's intelligence. It was quite necessary for him to cause that scene at Marguerite's in order to get out of it, because it was becoming true and natural between us, and what would someone like Pierre Indemini do with natural truth?

After long, morose considerings and hesitatings, Catherine made the decision to return to Vienna.

XIX

She landed in Vienna in September, on a Sunday evening. Almost happy. Will anyone tell her why?

And so she was here for her own pleasure or her own relaxation. She was setting herself free. She was quitting the movies. She was yielding, for x length of time. There would no longer be any question of Catharina. She was trying the adventure of a true friendship with Fanny. She was enjoying herself. She was moved that she would soon be seeing her again. At the same time she was fearful. Isn't any friendship an adventure when it is really pursued?

Her heart was pounding.

This was how they embraced on the inner stairway, and Catherine, put into an unfamiliar bed, fell asleep.

The Hohenstein house at the beginning of autumn was truly "Ruh-Land"—land of peace and quiet—with its masses of russet-red foliage, its gravel paths crisscrossed by gossamer, and, indoors, silence and warmth amidst the volumes of dark wood that reflected with melancholy the softness of the declining sky. At night, the double windows shut, an intelligent electricity came on in every spot where one might desire it. The first wood fires flamed without heating, for pleasure. One saw bouquets of late roses and asters, and in Fanny's small private room green plants were grouped under a brilliant Virginia creeper, which entered the open latticed windows from a balcony, stirred by the wind. Among the palms of her winter garden, Fanny also raised curious fishes, which waved pretentious black robes in the depths of their aquariums.

Catherine's room, whitewashed and completely peasant in its style, was restful as a spot for meditation. Not a single ornament. Whiteness and wood. The severity of the colors and the austerity of the forms was such that the bed, bed of birth, of love, and of sleep, was not unlike a coffin.

The room, facing south, was also gay, like a lark. Here Catherine read, smoked, curled up and stared into space, and daydreamed for hours at a time. "Here I am simply myself in search of myself. Well, we shall see."

She was delighted by the Hohensteins. The Hohensteins were delighted by her. Everything glowed. However:

They were a little different from those she had known the previous spring.

Fanny would say:

"My husband has not been so sad and is friendlier to me since you've been here."

Fanny Felicitas never failed to express, by one means or another, her joy at having Catherine.

She would continue:

"Have you noticed the silence between us? Yes?"

And absently, yet in order to elicit sympathy:

"It's funny, isn't it?"

She would offer pieces of information about Herr Hohenstein's state of health, like this: "His health, which had worried us so, would be almost restored now if it weren't for those persistent bouts of insomnia he has . . . He takes three or four tablets a night . . . but that's in connection with something else." They had separate bedrooms. Yet Baron Siegmund would answer Catherine that he had slept quite well, thank you.

When the baron was away, Fanny simply said he was traveling with his mistress. Catherine thought she had misunderstood.

"No, you didn't know? It's been going on for two years now, and it's pretty common knowledge."

And forgetting (thought Catherine) what she had confessed earlier—that there was great suffering between Herr Hohenstein and herself—Baroness Fanny spoke playfully and sang the praises of her husband's mistress, Fräulein K., typist.

"I know her. She came to see me. She sat there, just where you are."

And Fanny concluded with this remark:

"She's twenty years younger than I am."

Herr Hohenstein was always exceedingly courteous toward Catherine, courteous to the very limit courtesy can reach and still remain unobtrusive.

Guido, preparing for an examination in electrochemistry, paid no particular attention to Catherine. Except when, in honor of the Frenchwoman, he would introduce into the conversation his quite remarkable French puns.

He had a refrain—"That's amusing!"—and applied it with true wisdom to every event capable of causing suffering. Guido would laugh: "That's amusing!" He was gigantic, cunning, fresh as a rose.

The real enigma was Felicitas.

Her kindness, so warm and simple, her indulgence, but also the sorrowful expression in her bright eyes and their luster, the kisses she gave Catherine, intimated a great development of feeling and, even for a rather hard Frenchwoman maintaining all her composure, marked the imminence of a serious event.

XX

Fanny Felicitas asked Catherine to let her address her using *tu*, since she needed this sign of intimacy before beginning her story.

"I'll call you *tu* and you call me *tu*, all right? Say yes."

Fanny was visibly eager to use *tu*. She declared: "It's very simple, for a long time now I have been calling you *tu* to myself." Catherine had the greatest difficulty forcing herself to use the familiar form. Catherine made the mistake of joking:

"I feel like Susannah in the bath . . . "

Which she immediately regretted because Fanny Felicitas blushed with pleasure. Catherine felt Fanny's presence on her skin, so to speak. From then on she deliberately got herself tangled up in the forms of the verbs, she had to give up on it. Felicitas showed herself to be accommodating.

"Later," she said, "it will come of its own accord, won't it?"

On a winter's day there was already frost, and yet the vine still had a few mournful leaves. They were in Felicitas's little room. She was stretched out on a sofa whose material was split, Catherine was seated in an armchair that was likewise torn. Fanny, curling up her legs, tugged a chestnut-colored skirt down over her ankles. It was cold in the room. Here she obviously played at being poor. And except for her pretty head on a cushion, she looked like someone of no account.

Even though the setting seemed to promise a confidence, Fanny did not make up her mind to speak that afternoon; no doubt because Catherine was swinging her leg.

When Herr Hohenstein retired that evening, after some wearisome reflections about currencies and the problem of war, the two women found themselves at the same point, and Catherine was still swinging her leg.

"And," said Fanny, "if I wanted to tell you some things about my life this afternoon, it wasn't in order to reveal myself, or to make you love me, either. Just think, I am so eager to know . . . But I am an ignoramus. I don't know anything and I don't understand anything. Well, you can laugh if you like, Catherine, but I assure you, for example, I don't know . . . who Saint Paul is, or Plato? I have no personal knowledge of them." Behind her a small bookcase contained, handsomely bound, Suzo, Tauler, Angelus Silesius, Hölderlin, and Kleist. "You're looking at my books? *Someone* gave them to me, so I read them, I don't know any others. I like them very much."

Catherine had indeed noticed that where any intellectual thing was concerned Baroness Fanny affected to answer "I don't know."

"About myself I know even less. I spent a part of my life observing, it was so terrible; my ignorance remains complete. And yet, even though I may be *nothing*, I have an immense desire. In German we say *Sehnsucht*."

Catherine stares at the little woman with eyes full of anguish, pleasure, caresses, and she thinks she understands.

"One part of my desire is the need to express myself, to bring something out of myself, to see myself, myself in front of myself, do you understand? To create. Because if I managed to create a being of great beauty with what has happened to me within my private self, by observing the smallest detail, then I could realize: yes, of course it was this way and this way, and at that moment I would understand myself and I would no longer be a person without reality but a real woman; at last I would know my *Schicksal*, my fate. Do you believe I could make a script for a film using my life?"

The natural tendency, when a woman of the world takes you by surprise this way, is to laugh.

"I laughed because your life is certainly worth more than a film."

"With help from you, from you Catharina? You would write the film, you are such a great artist. You would act it."

Catherine, gently, "It's very hard to judge, Fanny, what your mistake is, and if . . . "

XXI

"If the subject matter exists? Here's the first episode, the beginning of a life, listen.

"Felicitas at nineteen. God, how pretty she is then! She lives in Vienna, and on the family estate at Selzthal where she was born, between her father, Professor Schomberg and her mother. Felicitas is as pretty as a robin and as innocent as the grass. I was cheerful, full of hope, I expected everything and I counted on having it all.

"Felicitas adores her parents, adores nature, adores pleasure. Her life is one great holiday. When there is no merry-making going on around her (as in the bleak House of the Teaching Sisters where she is deposited between the ages of sixteen and eighteen) she invents an inner fantasy still stronger. This young girl is well off, and she is unacquainted with petty concerns such as, for example, not leaving anything to chance as regards money and property. Felicitas has had three main ideas in her youth: fame in connection with her father, a man out of the ordinary; pleasure in connection with herself; and death in connection with her mother (she sees her die when she is sixteen and she is terrified by it).

"At nineteen, Felicitas meets Herr von Sonnenfels at a ball, an arranged meeting that produces the conventional results. Love at first sight, marriage. Felicitas becomes a Sonnenfels in the midst of general felicitations.

"Herr von Sonnenfels was a dozen years older than she. He was a vigorous and kind man, of sometimes difficult humor, not very sensitive, not very intelligent, exceedingly amorous. It is for this reason alone that Felicitas finds he is as handsome as the heavens.

"With Herr von Sonnenfels, Felicitas undergoes that experience which our grandmothers said was so important. She undergoes it, with success. M. de Sonnenfels rips rather brutally the curtain of a lie and Felicitas enters squarely into reality. Naturally this occurs during a trip, in Spain. Therefore very far away from my father, unfortunately. The house where they shut themselves up to love each other to the point of satiety is one of those little jail-like stone buildings, spare, painted dark blue, with a flat roof and iron balconies.

"Segovia.

"After three or four weeks Felicitas knows everything. She can proceed by herself henceforth, can live life in its entirety. At this point Guido Amering announces that he's arriving.

"Guido Amering was my husband's secretary. But Felicitas has made her own acquaintance with the traveler who is about to appear. Guido Amering was my friend well before Herr von Sonnenfels was my fiancé or even existed for me.

"Here is the earlier story with Guido Amering, which would have to be presented within a parenthesis. The Schombergs and the Amerings had been friends, Dr. Amering being a colleague of my father, Professor Schomberg, and during their adolescence Felicitas and Guido had sworn they would belong to each other. Time had passed, yet Guido Amering yearned for Felicitas and Felicitas (until shortly before the marriage) was with Guido in a moving and worn-out situation—do you understand?—after nocturnal meetings on the balcony (at Selzthal in summer) which put them to the test together. In our country, people are very fond of passions between youngsters, it's so charming, and generally does no harm.

"Of all this nothing remained, except that during my engagement, and as a consequence of the intervention of certain zealous persons, Guido Amering became the secretary of my future husband, who appreciated him very much. Guido Amering was much more intelligent than Herr von Sonnenfels. Everything forgotten on both sides, Guido had offered me his felicitations on the occasion of my marriage. Guido Amering was arriving in Segovia where we were staying, as secretary and for Herr von Sonnenfels's business affairs.

"I will go on.

"I myself dreamed only of obtaining the favors of my husband; I believed it, and it was impossible, you must understand, for me to believe anything else. This is what one will have to show, in images. It is so beautiful. Felicitas begs for pleasure, implores the attention, the gaze, of Herr von Sonnenfels. Enter

Guido. But it would also be necessary to show a rather strange Guido, poorly dressed on purpose to make a contrast with us, contemptuous, respectful. The Secretary. Three days after his arrival in Segovia we took him into town and everything went well. I visited the cathedral with him. Herr von Sonnenfels went horseback riding during this time, because he could not do without horses no matter where he was. Guido Amering returned home with Felicitas, cutting short the visit to the cathedral. Guido Amering went back up to his floor, Felicitas lay down toward evening, looking out the window at the magnificent landscape, wrapped in a black silk mantilla from the region. Guido Amering appeared behind her without transition, speaking of the balcony at Selzthal and of a rose garden where they used to embrace during the day; he asked for nothing, he lifted off the mantilla. I showed myself to him, I came immediately to the decisive gesture, and in the next minute I belonged to Guido, body and soul.

"Second episode. The newly married couple returns to Vienna. Guido Amering gone off somewhere to another place where my husband has sent him. Felicitas is beautiful, is sad, walks about in a dream. I remember a beggar in Barcelona who said to me, 'No need to be sweet as a fig in order to be black as cinders!' Naive Felicitas is no longer naive. And above all, she does not understand, she will never understand. One sees the arrival scene, the return to the bosom of the family, etc. But Guido Amering had only to lift his finger to have me again, as often as he might wish. Vienna horrifies me. I was twice married.

"Even though the game taxed her capacities, Felicitas could still put everything to rights: for she was happy with Sonnenfels, and frightened with Guido. Her love of Guido is surrounded by terror, perhaps by hatred. But Guido reappears in Vienna. His tactic consists in surprising Felicitas, in never being expected. Then Felicitas falls immediately and with all her weight, with a wonderful sweetness. Soon I could distinguish that I was smitten with Sonnenfels but in love with Guido. Instead of letting me go from one to the other, Guido Amering looks straight into my eyes with his extraordinary power of fascination and summons me to run away with him to a foreign country.

"Feeling that if he looked at me that way a second time I would obey him, I put off my answer to the next day and by letter I refused, I refused with a passion!

"There, Felicitas is alone. She feels something. What, she doesn't know, but something. Not enough perhaps? Or in harmony with the thing? Oh, Catharina, it is possible that the thing be accepted in advance, be desired—be *loved*, perhaps? No, my dear, it is not thus that one ought to understand my truth at that moment, but I'm forcing the drama, you understand? Let's say: I had a presentiment, and I was waiting to see if it would be true or not.

"Felicitas at the table, in Herr von Sonnenfels's presence, receives a letter: Guido Amering has killed himself. With a gunshot in the mouth.

"Felicitas who *knew it* is able to control herself until the end of the meal; it will not be said that *she* informed Herr von Sonnenfels of *this death*. Then she collapses in her bedroom, but there is no one in the world who can help her. The letter came from a stranger who was asked 'to inform Frau von Sonnenfels.' The thing happened far from Vienna and is not yet known. Felicitas is not at home to visitors. No release can take place, no coming to terms, not a tear. The next day, rejecting everything, hating herself, she goes in to her husband; he is taking his siesta. He sits up on his bed and looks at her half-asleep. Felicitas talks, talks like an idiot, without a pause she tells the whole story. She tells the story . . . to her father, she entreats him to console her. Her true father would be no help to her; it is up to the *second father* to understand; and won't the fact of the dead body deflect any offense? Herr von Sonnenfels listens and grows pale; in a nervous gesture he lets his monocle fall and puts it back. At last he points to the door, sends her back to her room, and himself leaves the house. He returns accompanied by one of his friends who is a lawyer, and the tale is resumed and proceeds, without interruptions, late into the night.

"At the end one would see Felicitas back in the home of her father, Dr. Schomberg, a few months later, poor as Job. Very quickly Herr von Sonnenfels repudiated her, having the marriage annulled in Rome.

"Within the space of a year I had been married, I had had a lover, who killed himself, I was divorced. Felicitas was twenty and a half years old. This is the beginning."

XXII

"Don't you think," Fanny added with a hint of wicked irony, "that this film could make a lot of money?"

"It isn't playable," said Catherine. "It doesn't exist."

Here's recompense for your complacency. Catherine, pacing the narrow confines of the room, immediately regretted her harshness, for Felicitas's eyes filled with tears.

Real tears, which first illuminated her pale blue eyes, then collected, flowed down her cheeks. Catherine, distraught: "Fanny, I'm a clumsy idiot."

Fanny, laughing-crying, shaking her head no. Catherine let herself go, kissed Fanny's hand; immediately red, excited, Fanny seemed recovered and ready to continue her tale.

"Felicitas is pregnant. The child arrives. The child resembles *both of them*. She calls it Guido. She carries over to this child all the love that is weighing her down, that she does not know what to do with, to her misfortune; and the love in itself is so strong that it has immediately put an end to the sorrows. Felicitas wants to live. But there is still something else to say."

(Fanny stands up and, walking to her secretary, changes appearance: this is a very feminine woman, whose soft, abundant body charms us.)

"While she was a young girl and quite happy, Felicitas dreamed of a child. She dreamed of having a child *for a child.* She dreamed with ardor and anguish of the feeling of feeling herself filled by the child, then of expelling it, of nursing it, of washing it. She had such a frenzy for a child that she cried in the tramway because she had gone to see a doctor in secret and she had learned that a woman *cannot* have a child without a man!

"With Guido, Felicitas begins her life of passion. It is in her character to demand much and more still. Every happiness she attains invites her to want a greater one, which will envelop the first. Thus, even today, do I prepare myself to demand *immensely* from Catharina! . . . Guido is sickly. Felicitas can't nurse him, she can only keep a supervising eye on the nurse. Guido is fretful. I adore him and I'm worried. I raise him alone, in an apartment in Vienna and during the summer at Selzthal. Yes, certainly! And in the same way that the child cries if one takes the breast from him and the first word he learns to say is 'more,' so I, his mother, still have, and have ever increasingly, the need to be given more."

(Fanny Felicitas showed Catherine an album covered in Cordova leather in which photographs of the same size were carefully pasted: one saw Guido every three months from his earliest days. In all his outfits, most often being held by his mother, on the occasion of all the holidays, all the trips, in her arms, standing, lying down, fairly often naked; there were a hundred or so different snapshots. Under the photographs, remarks like this: "Guido, contemplating the sky during the night of February 22, says: 'My God, I beg you, make some stars fall down for Guido!'"

"Guido says at five years: 'Mama told me that when I was born I had no head, no arms, no legs, nothing.'"

"Guido says: 'If the little earthworms were happy like me, they would all be glowworms.'")

"I ask for new proofs of love. The question of love is what I ask all around me. That's how I am. Even though, through everything, Guido occupied the most ardent part of my heart, I could not be satisfied with Guido alone. It's also that motherhood is a horrible fool's game, as love loses, loses, little by little, what it has created and what it loves. For fifteen years I practically did not take my eyes off Guido, and now I can't hope for more than to stay near him until he drives me away. Guido is certainly lucky, certainly lucky: for I have been and still am *all that he loves*.

"Felicitas needs many people in order to develop. She wants men, women. She is questing, she is seeking. She is about twenty-five years old. A great deal of life from all sides hurtles toward her.

"You, Catharina.

"You understand how it may be that one goes in search? If one carries within oneself *interest in life*. Amazing, handsome and young! Interest in life! And how all the others come toward you because they have the same interest in life! Fire for fire, life for life. And in the midst of all these figures of youth will come *the Chosen One* who by good fortune will explain the whole adventure!

"It would be easy to give each of the passions its own form, its character, to represent the different dream that each one embodies, each resulting, though, in the same sorrow, the same taste of ashes. 'Is this how it is, then? If it's this way, farewell.' If any man came within my reach I had to take his head in my hands just once and ask him, 'Is it you?'

"Among my loves of that time, there was also Annerl, my maid. A tall blond girl from Innsbruck, altogether magnificent, you know. It was she who led me to begin the *Freiluftgymnastik,* gymnastics in the open air, and I haven't stopped practicing it. My God, I feel small and wretched because I know that you will not want to do gymnastics with me! And then this past seems so paltry to me when I think that you are the one I'm telling it to."

Catherine made a face.

"Tell me, Felicitas, when you went from one man to another, were you happy or unhappy, I mean as you changed? Did you have the idea: I'm developing, this is my experience, I'm right; or the opposite: this is bad, I'm hurting myself?"

"But don't you see, if I do something it is good! I don't understand your question," said Felicitas with an enchanting smile.

"Several at the same time?"

"Not deliberately. If I had many friends, Catherine, it was because I had to. It wasn't for my pleasure. Searching for *the goal,* I had to approach men. I can't say it otherwise."

Catherine reflected.

About Felicitas? About herself?

"Let's come back to the death of your first friend. You had foreseen it, hadn't you? Amering?"

" . . . Yes."

"Well, what did you think—later?"

"I thought he could indeed die for me, because I loved him enough for that."

She is letting everything out of the bag. Catherine closes her eyelids.

She probably has to "play about" for a pitiful reason. "But why exhibit yourself so cruelly?" Catherine felt the beginnings of an attachment to, even an esteem for the little baroness, so red, so touching. At first there was a trick, but things are coming out, coming out . . .

Felicitas says: "Third episode."

XXIII

"On the mountain one day Felicitas meets Elisabeth. Elisabeth is married. To Baron Hohenstein.

"Here is Elisabeth's portrait. It is necessary that it be very beautiful.

"She was not tall; not small either. Slender, pliant, she reminded one of the stem of a plant. But look at her face, everything is there, have you ever seen anything more difficult to believe? An oval drawn as though through a fog or a dream. She really had this vaporous flesh, the photograph has nothing to do with it. Her chestnut hair, waved (very little), is arranged over her high and quite smooth forehead; in her hair one can see a part to the right, and a small flake above her left eye, a shiver on the other side. Her eyes, her eyes! But first look at her very straight nose; and her mouth is infinitely thin and pointed on both sides and it enters her cheeks through little hollows too supple to be dimples. Her eyes are the whole mystery of this person; they carry a veil; vague, they shine with an ardor and a sadness that fascinate. Isn't it so? Look at her neck, too, which has the beautiful motions of a swan's neck.

"She was there, a magnetic light radiated from her. You know, she was one of the most strangely pretty women in Vienna, and she was courted, to no avail, by everyone who saw her even once; but I say truly: to no avail. She was very virtuous. Her plain silk dresses were hardly open at all, and she always had long sleeves down to her wrists. Only on one evening were her shoulders visible, at a dinner that the press gave for Herr Hohenstein: Greek shoulders, sloping and quiet. No one understood her, in truth. That face was an open book with a hermetic meaning. One never again forgot it. I am the only one who read in that book.

"For what she really was went up from her like a smoke one couldn't grasp. There were plenty of people to judge her and say she was too sensual, or she was false, or she was cold and did not love her husband, or she was a melancholy hysteric—and all that had nothing to do with the reality. When she showed herself naked under the trees she was the most beautiful, with a natural beauty, that I have ever known, and the simplest in her soul. 'The woman's act' was superb in her, the classic dance in the presence of the sun and the sky."

Baroness Fanny took two photographs from the secret drawer of her small desk, and bent over with a great expansion of herself to show them.

"That's her and that's me."

In a meadow at the edge of a woods, two naked women whose nature is visible. The muscular bodies, face to face, were photographed during the dance and correspond symmetrically. Each, in profile, stands on one leg and flings the other leg back, and each has her two arms raised very high, the hands of one hold the hands of the other. Elisabeth is on the left, slender belly, long thighs, rather heavy breasts, and hair that flies away; Felicitas to the right forms the counterpart, a plump body, a rather erotic belly, and small breasts; one can't see Felicitas's face because she is not tipping her head back like her friend; Elisabeth's arms being longer, it is above Felicitas that the knot of the four hands is made. They are crowned with flowers in the ancient fashion.

"Very pretty," says Catherine.

The second photo is deplorably ugly. At the seaside, in front of waves, the ungracious creature smiling behind her sticky hair is Elisabeth, and she is pulling by the finger Felicitas, whose posterior parts are the most visible.

"Felicitas and Elisabeth!

"At first they have an aversion for each other—then poof!—suddenly that changes and now they feel an unsurpassable tenderness, desire, love; they cannot bear to be away from each other, separate for a minute, and after a week they are sleeping together.

"The greatest joys are bestowed on them.

"But we must explain our point of view. I find that love between two women is *so nice*. Compared to the other, which cruelly commits us, it is so good to leave us our freedom along with our femininity. It goes unnoticed. It is discreet, it can assume the appearance of virtue to deceive bad people. It is the flower under the grass. But if it is profound—then love has only one face! And will the love of women not be just as much love—I will say even more? We cultivate a more tremulous sensibility. Oh Catharina! They claim it is opposed to the other! No, no, no. I refuse to examine myself about this question of penchant. The world is great and passionate! I was not born to torment myself, I want to live. Yet I believe that Elisabeth was inclined much more than I, toward women.

"Do you agree with me, Catherine, that Love has only one face? Tell me."

"Yes, that's probably true," says Catherine, prudently.

"The two women in this photograph are in love for three years. There is not a fog or a cloud. It is as smooth as the sky in the month of August. Nothing, you understand, could tarnish their purity; everything, on the contrary, enters into the pure order; and why? Because the source is pure at its origins. Felicitas has never *loved* a man; now she loves. Elisabeth has sides to her that are sharp, frightening; Felicitas is flexibility itself: Elisabeth orders and Felicitas obeys. Felicitas lives this way with her friend Elisabeth Hohenstein. From their pairing emerges a tenderness that does everyone good, and most of all Baron Hohenstein, who is tied to Felicitas by a strong friendship. Their happiness seems eternal, when—

"All of a sudden Elisabeth becomes sad . . .

"Listen, my Catharina," says Fanny, abruptly changing her

tone, "it is two o'clock in the morning, let's go to sleep!"

"No," says Catherine, "the next part."

"What, you want more of this? For me it's easy to go night after night without sleep. But you."

"Go on!"

"Well, all right. . . . Really? Catharina dear?"

"Go on. I'm listening."

"*Elisabeth becomes sad.* She has had two attacks of this sadness before, when she was a girl, when she remained in her bed for nearly a year; then with Herr Hohenstein in the beginning. Apparently it is hysteria. She changes completely, physically and mentally. At certain hours she seems like her own mother, and something even older. She is not sick, I mean her body is not sick; only her soul, the soul alone. Felicitas knows nothing about this illness, which takes the following form this time: Elisabeth, without ceasing to pursue her life on the outside, is no longer Elisabeth on the inside and no longer has her personality.

"Her recollection is gone, no memories. Her senses, dead. She lives like a machine. Move her and show her what role to play, she plays it. She smiles only at my son Guido. Herr Hohenstein does not seem alarmed. But Felicitas! How can she live? Elisabeth's feelings are withered plants. She is hidden cunningly behind herself. And the happiest love stretches, in a few days becomes a painful thread, and snaps."

"Wasn't it really you who were there, wicked Fanny, *as you were for Guido Amering?*"

"What do you mean, me? I adore her."

"Go on."

"But it's over soon. If I take pity on her, she communicates her sorrow to me, she knows very well how to do it, or she stares at me with her eyes like two bolts of lightning and makes me cry. Above all, she refuses the consolation I can give her. Tenderness is poison for her. When she stops crying, she is ferocious. I discover that her only attachment is to Hohenstein. She follows him like a dog. One day she is feeling a little better and she contemplates Felicitas with an air of goodness, hypocrisy, decency, so awful—which means: I have seen nothing, heard nothing, nothing has happened, go away—that poor Felicitas, in tears, leaves the house.

"They depart for Africa. She and he. A trip he had arranged hastily. She was to enjoy a long rest on the sea. I, in such pain I could have cried out, waved my handkerchief on the dock . . .

"When I saw Herr Hohenstein again he told me this.

"They are out at sea off Dakar, on the boat. She is recovered. She thinks of me all the time. She talks about me to Hohenstein but she doesn't write to me."

"I understand," says Catherine. And she stands up. "Let's act out the scene. Did Elisabeth know the end of the story with Amering?"

"Of course."

"I am *her*. I am lying on the deck. I am in a deck chair." Catherine lies down.

Felicitas begins pacing up and down the parlor, her eyes shining as though she had a fever.

Felicitas: "You say nothing true to Hohenstein. There you are, completely recovered, but you still imitate the illness a little to keep a distance, a density between you and him."

Catherine played it to the hilt with mimicry and mute speech. In the Ruh-Land parlor appears a figure whom no one knows, intense, enigmatic, who, by projecting all sorts of black rays, interferes with the warm sun of the sea, and who watches, watches, watches the point that is there beyond the deep. What point? What she will be—what she will feel—or will not feel—eternity . . . the void . . . in a minute or two, when her body, when she, will be no more than a bag of water under the waves . . . Everything is decided now, and it is *for Felicitas*.

"Baron Hohenstein asks you if you would like to go for a stroll."

"If you like" (with a weary air).

Wonderful gesture from Catherine! (What is important is to be alone now.)

"After the second turn around the deck you let go of Herr Hohenstein's arm and you go into the lavatory, with which you are familiar. There everything is estimated, surveyed, the bolt, the porthole, the height."

Catherine acts.

"Hohenstein is at the door and he is waiting."

Felicitas plays Hohenstein: she knocks at the door, listens, becomes impatient.

Felicitas utters a cry.

"Hohenstein sees *the shadow* pass across some frosted glass in the passageway. It is you, through the porthole. You are dead."

THE DISCOVERY OF REALITY

XXIV

During the three months that followed, Fanny and Catherine did not leave each other. As though they were diving together under the sea. Talking a good deal, also contriving long silences, certain silences. Revealing themselves to each other, but Fanny much more; the appearance of her story remained the same, less a confidence than an exhibition.

In the boudoir, not entirely closed (open on Guido's studio), or a corner of the hall with the historic furniture, or on the light-colored rugs of the parlor, or by Fanny's bed in the morning (sitting at the foot), curiously absorbed withal but stirred up again and full of interest, Catherine had reeled up what Felicitas was unreeling. Felicitas was now unreeling the worst; Catherine was not paying attention to the quality. This is what is called diving together. Under the sea. Sometimes Catherine would walk alone in the half-German, half-Italian city with snow on the cornices of the palaces, and, uneasy, would go over everything again in her head, without understanding. She could still take stock of it for herself, but not for Fanny. About Fanny she knew a lot—and nothing. The more Fanny allowed herself to be seen, the more Fanny kept her secret. And suddenly Catherine, with a crazy fear, asked herself, what was hidden beneath? To put it another way, she felt attached to Fanny by an indefinable force, so much so that Fanny might possibly keep Catherine at Ruh-Land in her present state of emotion as long as she wished. But she, Catherine, had spoken almost not at all. Anyway, how much room was left after Fanny's display of sentiment? If Catherine felt mentally the way she was physically in this street, unsure of herself and floundering along, it was therefore because of her own misery and, in the heart of that personal misery, because of a disturbance overstimulated by Fanny's own disturbance.

The pleasure of love lasts but an instant,
The sorrow of love . . .

"And also, why leave the profession (however grim it may be)
that makes you happy, that sets you free? Why? In order not to
go on living alone. In order to try life out: we'll see what you can
do. But once Catharina is no more, life becomes worthless. I am
immobilized here, welcomed into a rich house, without a penny.
I'm hanging about. And *the other thing,* which I have trouble seeing clearly, *is taking me even farther down.* What is it? I am like
Felicitas, we are two of a kind . . . ill from an old love."

She returned late to Ruh-Land. Everyone was waiting for her,
entertained her around the peaceful, sumptuous table.

XXV

Catherine had, then, learned this continuation:

After Elisabeth's death, presented as accidental, Fanny had
married Siegmund Hohenstein, and this was not the least surprising thing in her story.

Self-interest at several levels had led her to make this marriage.
On the realistic level, Hohenstein had a name, a fortune, and
importance in society, Fanny's too many successive lovers having
cost her a fair amount of esteem and, in the way of money, "almost
all the capital her father had given her." On the level of feelings it
was very complicated. Fanny had found this indirect means of
appeasing Hohenstein's resentment against her by managing to
insinuate herself into Elisabeth by a path of affection, by almost
appropriating the memory of Elisabeth; the least possible love
had been lost, since she loved and looked after the man her
friend Elisabeth had left unhappy.

The baron appeared to be in love, having changed from an
unhappy man into a happy one. Fanny Felicitas, then, is perform-

ing miracles; and after several months (from success to success) the round of lovers begins again, without Felicitas having "anything to reproach herself with." Catherine had been startled by this simple phrase, as when someone touches you on the arm and you awaken from a dream, but Felicitas's smile resting on her had benumbed her again.

There are fewer lovers, she chooses them more carefully. She believes in the necessary lover more than she loves, and she cannot do without the "possibility" that a new lover offers, since pleasure is the only outcome allowed to develop. Felicitas withdraws, each time despised, and despises each man more beforehand.

"Why are you telling me these stories?" asked Catherine.

"So that you will know very clearly how one can despise men."

Fanny, having gone back to the Catholic faith under Hohenstein's influence (even though there is Jewish blood in her), arranges all this with some difficulty: either she moves away from the church for a time or she does penance and continues. Herr Hohenstein knows about almost all his wife's intrigues, but whether out of charity or wisdom or lack of energy, in practice he is indifferent, though only on the following conditions: that the social facade be carefully maintained and the affair come to an end. The lovers are generally friends of his. Herr Hohenstein stands back. Fanny is the center of a male circle, and Fanny's previous men are not one another's enemies. Hohenstein is very tender toward Felicitas, tender and ceremonious; their intimate relations had ceased after two years, and the baron sometimes takes a mistress in town who distracts him from his worries but has no importance.

Fanny Felicitas described the "pied-à-terre" she herself had in the apartment of a poor but respectable family: "it's very ugly, very uncomfortable." Here she would receive her friend at eleven-thirty or noon. This was the best moment, after the morning errands and before the late Viennese lunch served at Ruh-Land around two o'clock. Fanny gave Catherine many erotic details. She also confessed that during her pleasure she liked to have herself called "Deo gratias," because this was what a sacristan of Selzthal had nicknamed her when she was little—a blasphemy on Fanny's part of which she was not very distinctly aware. The more unhappy Felicitas was, the more proportionately excited she was.

XXVI

No one in that place who did not have his problem. Nor was Baron Siegmund's "problem" unimportant. Guido's problem could yield an entire tragedy. How many conflicts brought together in this peaceful land! Catherine believed she was learning psychology. She did not rediscover what she had experienced before, a civilization without problems, where money and the ownership of bodies solve all questions. Now here, as each was familiar with the needs, the faults, the misadventures, the mistakes of the other, all acted continually on each other and remained together without changing anything and without hating one another. A combat of discreet monsters; victories and defeats have no meaning.

Hohenstein was attached to his pseudo-son by a strong and bizarre affection, and Fanny pointed it out to her, saying, "He is in love, isn't he?" This affection of the baron for Guido dated from Guido's eleventh year, in other words, from the time when Herr Hohenstein ceased to be his wife's lover. Herr Hohenstein communicated to Guido von Sonnenfels his ideas, his plans, referred the paper's dealings to him, and discussed political economy with him. This Guido, indifferent to a woman's attractions (he was left quite unmoved by Catherine's breasts under her blouse, the line of her calf), was by reason of his very deficiency when it came to loving endowed with a maturity full of experience.

Let us look at it more closely. The relationship between the baron and Guido guarantees the endurance of the second Hohenstein marriage. Like a new beam introduced under the house, it prevents disastrous cracks from widening. If it were not for "the boy," wouldn't Herr Hohenstein have asked Felicitas, in his polite, contemptuous voice, to consider divorce, something Felicitas would reject indignantly with deep-seated rage, for she will never allow *this to happen for the second time?* Thus do the attachments, the restraints, the animosities operate.

What is more, Fanny's system with her son is extraordinary.

One could say that it consists in always giving him life but always taking it back from him. She babies him perpetually in order to keep him wailing. She transmits reality to him while taking from him the means to feel it.

She has established a scrupulous domination over him. That domination is of the same nature as her domination over the objects or the money in the house; or her domination over Guido is the beginning of her domination in general. She looks at him often. She looks at him in a significant manner. Dreamily, like a poor fiancée. With a caressing and ironic eye. Or manifesting a feminine experience of life so profound that her maternal authority no longer has room to show itself afterward. She laughs with him, little laughs without value and without any necessity, which give such pleasure because they imply so much. She does not leave him in peace. She plays the lover, but the lover of eternal promises and serious efforts. She also plays the absurd mother. She binds him through a feeling of grotesqueness: I am the colossal son of this little enamored woman. She is prepared for anything. She will do anything so that Guido may remain Guido. She will succeed in this.

No doubt she particularly loves her son's virginity: she intends to lie down across any path that leads from her son to a woman. She confesses it, she knows it. "No, I don't want him to know a single woman!" Does she herself not bring woman to her son in a desexualized and salutary form? Who knows? Nor does she mind irritating Guido by the display of a horrible femininity, her own. Everything must contribute to the goal if she has been able to carry out this operation: that her son love her no matter what harm is done.

An example of the truth flung forth and retained: Felicitas telling her son "without lies" about her life, something she had done—she said to Catherine—since he was old enough to understand. If she declared to Guido, "I have a lover," she was at the same time depriving him of the meaning of that word. Guido had his refrain—"That's amusing!"—which he reproduced constantly, and he showed his splendid teeth, the teeth of a young Negro. It was in Guido's presence that Catherine had heard tell of a young man, mysterious, far superior to all the others, with whom Felicitas was now involved. But if Felicitas, having to explain one of her midday meetings, said to Guido, "I'm going to go for a walk with him," it might happen that Guido would answer with his most cunning air, "Since you go for walks so often I will follow you on my bicycle!"—and Felicitas, laughing until she cried, would embrace her dear son.

XXVII

Thus did she spiral downward. Her condition was gentler, more foolish, more inert. Something was brewing, however, which she could not have named. Something was lying in wait at the street corner, for finally . . . They were also waiting for the spring. It did not want to come. Nothing served any longer, that year, for anyone. They found themselves at such a low ebb that they yawned in front of everyone. The baroness and Catherine were *intimate friends*. Apart from a certain dizziness in the morning, Catherine scarcely noticed her state. They ate, they digested while drinking tea and whiskey. They smoked, they slept. They talked nonsense. They were always together. No new person entered Ruh-Land—"I'm a hermit," Fanny had said—and they went out (the two of them) only for their "constitutional," as the English call it, in a coat of leather or fur, along roads where the walkway for pedestrians, protected by romantic trees, overlooks the cars. They found themselves in mountainside forests. They were light-hearted, and they were bored.

No one, as we say, came to Ruh-Land, except for two dinner guests who did not have much more reality than the furniture in the museum: Fanny's old governess, who was fat, had a small head, and an indubitably fierce air, and (on first and third Thurs-days) Dr. Schomberg, honorary professor of penal law, whose consistency was little by little evaporating into winks and witti-cisms. Since they both liked a good deal of sleep, they left Ruh-Land at nine o'clock. Their visits only underscored Fanny's soli-tude, and during the meals Herr Hohenstein had carried his pleasant moroseness to new heights.

Gone. Fanny would head for the light switches. She would put on "the soft light." She would sit down facing Catherine, sometimes on the floor. She would always begin this way: "I did-n't see you this morning . . . " in a tone of reproach so tender, so naive, that Catherine would laugh, either excited or annoyed; goaded. This was their conventional language. They started in on it together. They would chatter until the middle of the night. About vague subjects. Laughing often and a great deal. They showed each other their likes and dislikes, their desires, their fears. They told each other dreams they had had.

Yet one time the baroness displayed an intense uneasiness: "What should one do if one knows what God demands of us?"

"Is it nice?" answered Catherine, thinking of something else.

"How should one obey?" the baroness went on, for she was in no doubt about the reality of the divine warning.

"Well, what is it?"

With real modesty in her expression, the baroness told her she knew God's desire with respect to her: it was that she should have no more physical relations with a man.

"And with a woman?" said Catherine nastily, to provoke.

Fanny blew the smoke from her cigarette up to the ceiling. "You're not at all religious."

XXVIII

Catherine, still in a sort of rumination, was sitting in the Opera Café. Fanny had insisted that she wait for her there, "but we won't stay there, and we shall go off into the town together." Arriving at the café at about ten o'clock, Catherine saw nothing.

Fanny appeared at eleven-thirty.

Wearing a fancy hat, very smartly dressed, she was hardly recognizable. She seemed fairly nervous and in a hurry, as though she had something to do. Outside, she said to Catherine, "Give me your arm." In general she did not talk this way. But there were too many people and cars, and they walked separately.

The event inside Catherine: I am sitting in this dirty Opera Café. I'm holding a big French newspaper in my hand. There is almost no one here, a few habitués. The other woman comes up (to me) and in a Jewish accent says, "Haven't you forgotten something?" "No," I answer, "no," and I go on reading my newspaper. She comes up a second time; irritated, I put down my newspaper and recognize my dear friend. Felicitas. She is carrying a traveling bag on which she has glued

For ladies only

and she is really disgustingly well dressed. "Stir yourself and come on, now," she says, "I'm heading home." I leave the Opera Café. She has never spoken to me in this tone. Or taken me by the arm. It's very unpleasant for me, but I *must* be patient. Through streets that I don't know we arrive in front of a house. Here she draws out a bunch of keys and detaches the smallest, saying, "This is the one to my bag. Since I have *confidence* in you" (what a look she gives me! with a wink, even, it's unbearable) "I'm going to give it to you. But be careful that it doesn't fall into my husband's possession: it opens my handbag. My husband is very indiscreet, he pokes into all my affairs, so I am entrusting you with my little key." I say to her, "I don't understand a word of what you are saying." She repeats the same sentences word for word, shows the bag "for ladies only," and leaves me in the street, the key in my hand, and disappears into this unfamiliar house.

Catherine was in fact on the sidewalk of Mariahilferstrasse. Fanny had been swallowed up by house no. 103. The house was the one where she had her pied-à-terre. Catherine shivered. It's too much! Let's leave right away. And Catherine stood petrified in the street, transfixed by a psychological revelation: the baroness's desire—is settling—now—on Catherine.

Yes, first this, then that, the progress of feelings, in effect. From the beginning this was the goal. Why of course. Why it's obvious. "You will do everything. You will save everything. You will pull me by the hand. . . . " I didn't believe it. Oh, I was so foolish.

"Ladies only" is explicit. She is showing me the way to the pied-à-terre.

Take the train tonight! I don't have a penny. But who is in there waiting for her? The other. It's too much. And God who is asking her not to have any more relations with a man! Horrible. But also, she is afraid of losing that lover! Did you see how she hurried up the stairs? Well? Well? Well what does she want from me? Not that I should take his place. That an adventure with me should give new heat to her intrigue with him. No, that's stupid. Or that all three of us . . . Hell.

And what was Catherine holding in her fingers? She looked. The key to the bag, the little nickel-plated key.

XXIX

My God, no! It's not the first time that that disgusting proposition has been made to me.

In Paris I have often noticed that more women than men follow me in the street. More women than men seem to be offering me their lives. And these women are always very feminine, feminine like Felicitas, more feminine than I am. Am I, then, a magnet for these looks? Is it my fault? But is it possible? A woman is repugnant to me from a sexual point of view! My God, my God, what in the world have I done to poison all love in myself?

She remembered a factory girl in Tourc . . . accosting her in a shady backstreet at dusk, saying to her the word for the thing, and blushing to the eyes she was so infatuated. (She had the face of a decent girl.) Shimmers and light touches. In studios, too; Servandoni had wanted that for a time after Pierre left.

I am the devil, said Catherine.

And to merit her name she spat.

"But with Fanny it was inevitable!"

"I beg your pardon?"

"I say: with Fanny it was bound to happen. You had already known that for a long time."

"I knew it? I? I'm dumbfounded."

"You're kidding me."

"'Not at all. This depravation of the friendship did not necessarily have to happen."

"'This depravation of the friendship! This depravation of the friendship!'"

"This disgustingness of your tricks."

"These lies of your tongue."

"Fanny has needs, and she let you know about them fairly early on."

"What does that prove to me?"

"I may add that you knew (what is called knowing, knowing inwardly) that Fanny's friendship is *always* like that."

"What she wanted from you."

"And when you realized it, I could tell you the precise day, well before the satchel business, what did you do? You found that desire *amusing*."

"That's not true!"

"You slept peacefully in the bed belonging to that house, since the bed belonging to that house was at that price."

"That's not true!"

"You spent your time tangling, untangling, retangling the ins and outs of all that."

"She was able to believe that this would work since you were so accommodating, so willing to listen to her stories."

"But really, come now, didn't there exist between her and me something clean, nice?"

"Since you had her in the palm of your hand, you assumed the noble role of the moral conscience."

"And what, according to you, was the reason for my willingness to listen to the details?"

"People certainly look at obscene photographs: it amused you."

"How you accuse me!"

"Ten times less than I should."

She had put the key on a table near Felicitas's bed. The key had been taken back, without a word being said. The baroness seemed more reserved since the business of the bag. The only allusion, perhaps?—she kissed Catherine's hand inside the palm.

Catherine began to talk vaguely about her departure.

Never had Ruh-Land been more tender, never more persuasive its counsel to live happily. The heat was forming in the sky and the lawn was covered with daisies. The gravel shone. They were comfortable in rattan chairs. Fanny, with the help of the gardener, gave fish of several races their freedom again in the open water of the pool, reserving the others for warmer weather. They prepared the bottom with algae; elsewhere earth was being turned over where the plants from the greenhouses would be set out. Catherine was reading German poets, dressed in pale colors and sitting in the sun. Fanny came up to her: "What are you reading? Show me." While in the distance exploded the baritone of young Guido, working on his technique and sending forth a melody by Schubert. It was a trap of pleasantness. "Springtime puts me to sleep. Why should I go? After all, I like Fanny very much." And Herr Hohenstein begged Catherine to stay on through the summer.

XXX

An "obviously devil-inspired" desire was goading her to look in the other direction. The demon of perversity wanted her to come in contact with a clear reality finally, to unmask the silent protagonist, and it seemed to her that afterward she would be able to leave.

Felicitas, secretive life whose center shifts constantly but whose surface is painted over with a veneer of goodness and falsehood, what lover have you managed to preserve?

She returned to Mariahilferstrasse and found the house again. Sinister, of blackish gray cement. Catherine possessed only one vague fact about the pied-à-terre: it was on the fourth floor. Speaking the language almost not at all, one cannot find out anything about anyone. Fanny comes here every two days.

Catherine established herself in a small café on the ground floor of the building next door. The first time, it was impossible to be near the window, the attempt had failed, she left before the appointed hour. Two days later she was beside the window, but the hour came and went without her seeing Felicitas.

Catherine looks out between the yellow curtain and the wall made of heavy waxed wood with hooks for clothes. She is bored. She is a little disgusted with herself. She is very determined. She must get out of this.

The third time this is what happened. Felicitas passed by (right against the window), Felicitas brushed against Catherine's face. Her luck continued, because Felicitas passed again in the same way at twelve-forty, hailed a taxi, and drove off in it.

Catherine enters the house. The stone staircase occupies a very large oval well. Upon entering one receives the impression of bourgeois ominousness. Here is Catherine at the first floor. The doors are grimacing, divided into several parts by decorative forms in the floral style, and each one has a little brass peephole through which one can get a look at a stranger; the doormat is attached to the wall by substantial chains.

Catherine climbs the stairway with a deliberate firmness and without being able to tell where she is going. Her body is tense. But her mind (how idiotic it is) is completely empty. She has no plan. Up above she will ask for Baroness Hohenstein. Second floor. Beating of her heart. Stop.

Yes, it is Catherine's body that is conducting the experiment and leading her here. Her eyes look, peer about. At the third floor she sees that there are two doors. Her gaze goes from one to the other. A small line has formed in Catherine's smooth forehead, in the middle; her lashes keep moving, her nostrils, too, and all of this is following from a distance the activity of her heart. Her lips are tightly pressed together. Another moment. She chooses: the door to the left. Her entire body is engaged. Catherine has an obscure memory of having lived through this scene at an earlier time.

She climbs up and draws near.

A living room . . . another life . . .

Then we see Catherine's face change as if a light were inside it.

Her face changes; her lips open, part, her teeth appear, and her eyes are closed. Her head bows and even rests against the wall. Her body stops moving. Then she is staring wide-eyed. An immense heat rises and settles in her cheeks. A vapor of confusion. Her eyes are still so wide open that her gaze disappears and vanishes. The muscles of Catherine's legs lift her one more time. She walks like a woman halfway in a faint. The lover is there in the open door. The lover is—

Pierre Indemini.

Pierre does not move. Catherine does not move. A very long moment goes by, then Pierre says (but barely): "It's you, Catherine. I was waiting for you."

And they go back up into the pied-à-terre.

HAPPY DAY

XXXI

Pierre Indemini leaves the Douxmaison house where he has ditched Catherine. His heart somber and light, he has a replacement affair with Servandoni that does not last. He can't stand it anymore. Paris exasperates him; he goes off. He liquidates the family property, which, as long as it is not sold, binds you to the land; he is free. He travels over a part of America, from which he immediately flees. He rests for a brief time in the England of the universities, then in Germany, and here he is in Vienna; from here he embarks on an immense metaphysical voyage . . . He takes a good many women in his arms . . .

Catherine looks at him.

He is still called Pierre Indemini. He still has that charming, ungainly air. The same blond hair, the same face expressing his inner life, one would have to say that the flesh was deep there.

. . . He takes a good many women in his arms. He loses his bearings in a succession of real love affairs. Beautiful or deceitful, true or futile. He leads two lives. But his mind's adventure is still more astonishing. He accepts the suffering that forms the counterpart. He is carried by his bodily beauty and the active humor of his intelligence. He regularly works eight hours a day. Disregarding the vulgarity of the business world, the intellectual vulgarity, the artistic vulgarity of our time, he becomes one of the ten minds that can follow the works of Sir M. R. on the philosophy of mathematics, and he himself is concerned with problems situated between logic and biology.

"Yes? Truly?" thinks Catherine. "To such an extent as that?"

They haven't exchanged a word.

. . . Having come to Vienna as a foreign professor, Pierre Indemini meets, at the home of an unusual Jewish philosopher, the Baroness Fanny Felicitas Hohenstein.

Baroness Fanny is for him the most extraordinary type of the "body" he has ever seen. Now, in the crisis of his thinking that is

beginning at about this time, characterized by a very great preoc-
cupation with the problem of *death,* Fanny Felicitas is the body,
the heat, the consolation as necessary to Pierre Indemini as bread.

Catherine indicates that "they can chat."

XXXII

"You're . . . staying in Vienna?" says Pierre.

"Yes, in Vienna. I've been here six months. And you?"

"Two years."

"Two years. And . . . you're Fanny's friend?" Glances around
her at the sinister pied-à-terre.

"Fanny's friend. Shall I ask you the same question?"

"Oh, you may. Fanny's friend."

"I know a lot about you, as Fanny's friend."

"Really. I knew nothing at all about you."

"Admit that life is incredible, disconcerting."

"It is."

"But I had only just guessed your identity. For a long time you
were disguised under the features of a Swede."

Catherine smiles. Pierre smiles. They smile.

Then they give themselves over to silence. Pierre lights a cigarette after having opened his pack in front of Catherine, who
declines.

"All the same, it's a bit much!" Catherine resumes.

"The how and the why," Pierre rejoins laconically.

Another silence. They give up talking.

"You've been her lover for two years?"

Pierre opens his mouth to answer, but a laugh comes forth.
Explosive, pointed, violent, painful laughter. It is forbidden to
laugh like that. Laughter. The demon. Uncontrolled laughter.
Pierre's laughter soars into the air and falls back on all sides. His

gaiety makes a noise that can be heard all through the house.

He strides about the apartment. Catherine is leaning back against the bedstead.

"Forgive me for laughing like that, it was idiotic."

But he starts in again.

No, no one has the right to laugh in that way. The meeting has struck terror into Catherine's heart, but the laughter's effect is murderous.

That laughter kills visible and invisible creatures, rolls the past into a lump as though it were dough or mud, debases the sacred image one forms, wounds God. However, Catherine must restrain herself, restrain herself: it will get to me, and I will laugh with him.

Pierre stopped abruptly. He ran his hand over his forehead.

"Catherine, you did a lot for me."

"Did I now! Well!" She—who doesn't understand.

"I'm not the same man who left you."

"Actually, I can see that." (A little worse.)

The world was slipping, slipping over Catherine's fixed gaze. It was tumbling into vertiginous depths; it was abandoning the horizontal, in horror. The fact that he was addressing her with the intimate *tu* had that effect.

I am lost. I still love him.

"Catherine, this morning it is given to me to see. When I left you, I was a scoundrel who didn't know what he was or what he cared about."

"Take care. Else you may see too clearly!"

Her turn to laugh—like a knife thrust. Here, take it!

"Unfortunately," said Pierre. "It is true indeed that I do not cut a very fine figure in this place and at this hour. But I have worked upon that bad heart. Something quite different. You must know."

Where is it, where is the door to this place? So that I can get out. Where is the door?

"I have the weakness of a plant, I'm sensitive to every pleasure, I don't mend my faults, I commit others, etc. A person holds me, I know what that person may claim, she *thinks* she holds me, Catherine."

"Identifying mark: nothingness."

"Hmm?"

"I am having silly ideas. I was thinking of my passport."

"Catherine, I beg you to stay, not to leave." He is using the formal *vous* again.

She feels his distress. She becomes stronger.

"I should tell you, anyway, that no one has talked to me about you."

"During these five years I have taken some steps forward. If I have taken a single step in the direction of myself, I owe it to you entirely."

" . . . Is that so?"

"I left you with the illusion that the break was painless for me. You may have thought that I did not carry away with me either sorrow or memory."

"But I had no *illusion* at all! I did not think anything! I did not attribute any sorrow to you!" (She would like to hurl a "my dear fellow" at him; that would be wicked, it's burning her mouth.)

"After that, thinking of you often, in an odd way, and, I now know, with the ulterior motive of finding you again someday for the second time, I built up a whole structure against such cowardly instincts. There."

Catherine can no longer contain herself.

"And—you exercise these lofty qualities here?"

Image of Felicitas capering about in her slip an hour earlier.

"Have the kindness to understand."

"But!" shouted Catherine at the top of her lungs. "Explain, then, explain! You—and Felicitas—is it possible?!"

"Very possible, alas."

"Well, then, good-bye."

"You won't leave Vienna."

"That's my concern."

"You won't pay me back the harm that I did you."

"Why not?"

"The moment is more serious than either of us, in this scene, can imagine. I'm approaching the end, Catherine."

"What end? Are you perhaps going to die for her?"

" . . . and locked inside a great fear, perhaps on the threshold of something else, I need you. Do you understand me? Need you. Help me."

"Help you."

XXXIII

The next day, at morning tea, Felicitas herself buttered Catherine's toast.

"*You made a great many visits* yesterday, dear woman, didn't you?"

Catherine bristled. Let it all blow up right now if it wants to. But with Felicitas how could life ever have blowups? Felicitas added, threatening saucily with her forefinger, "*I know about it. And I am forgiving you this very instant!*"

"But I have nothing that needs to be forgiven!"

"My Catharina, let's be frank, let's be calm. Let's be two *doves*. You knew Pierre Indemini?"

"Very well. And I saw him again."

"You were formerly . . . Oh, how funny it is!" Felicitas murmured. "It's delightful."

"Yes," said Catherine, putting all her sadness into that *yes*.

Felicitas waited a moment.

"Say that it's a pretty thing. A fairy tale."

And in fact Catherine's empty cup, which she set down on the saucer, shatters.

"Very pretty. Indeed."

"You are upset, Catharina."

"I? Not at all."

"Now tell me the story."

"I shall tell nothing at all."

"But you're not going to be mean . . . to me, to me, poor Felicitas? I don't want that. I'll make them gentle, those terrible eyes. Because I love them . . . "

Felicitas lays her gracious hand on Catherine's chest; Catherine feels oppressed, short of breath.

"*You know* that you are more than he is? You don't know that?"

Catherine goes back to calling her *tu*.

"My intention was to let you know about my meeting with Indemini, you may believe that."

"I can guess what it was like. And anyway, isn't he like all men, can he keep quiet?"

"He told you! . . . "

"No, of course not, my dearest, and besides, I haven't seen him since then."

"So?"

"Let's set that aside. But listen, what is happening seems to me so astonishing, supernatural, providential, don't you think so too?"

Catherine, shocked: "I don't understand."

"It was him, wasn't it, Catha, that you talked to me about with so much reticence, once in the garden? Who hurt you? Him?"

"Him."

"Oh, how funny it is! Very beautiful. Very dramatic."

"I can't bear any more of this," said Catherine.

"Oh, extraordinary! Extraordinary!"

The baroness clapped her hands.

" . . . Now I feel justified. I loved him very much. I see that he is the best man in my life. He never said a word to me about you. I swear it. Our relationship has had a touching history just about from the start. He arrived in Vienna poor and very weak in health. I singled him out right away. He is very intelligent, isn't he; he is superior. I believe also that I kept him from dying, that boy."

"From dying?" Even though the word no longer surprises her, is already familiar, Catherine bites her lip until it bleeds.

"Pierre Indemini," Felicitas begins, "is obsessed by death. He thinks only about death. He relates everything that life gives him to this terrible idea, that he, along with the thing which is life, is going to disappear forever. He is a materialist. He does not have, as I do, the consolations of the Catholic religion. It wasn't up to me to convert him, but I have been able to give him the living security he asks for (how can I say it nicely?), the warmth of life in good harmony with life. In my arms he has had the peace we all need. He is better now."

Catherine is silent.

"Do you understand what I'm trying to express?"

Felicitas remains unflustered.

"You certainly knew, Catharina, the saving feeling I have for *you*. It's the passionate hope for a metamorphosis: you are my indomitable heroine, and together we are going to kill the monster of ancient times! Well, what a heaven-sent coincidence. One day I met and loved Pierre Indemini; but you had loved Pierre Indemini before me! It is therefore you whom I was seeking to love in him! And without wanting suddenly to lose Pierre (whom I still love), I feel that I love Pierre to the extent that he was the one leading me in some obscure way to you!

"Now. What about you? Do you still have a feeling for him?"

Catherine: "I'm not saying anything. It is Pierre who will speak between the two of us."

A cloud passed over Felicitas, but a cloud that resolved into light, into a smile. She drew Catherine to her, despite her resistance, until Catherine's head lay against her shoulder.

"Everything will be good, my lovely one, everything will be good, we don't want to hurt anything, force anything; everything will be very good."

XXXIV

Catherine, far from Paris, was writing to Marguerite de Doux-maison. Several letters from that period:

I'm writing to you what I can, the main thing, and I confess, it's quite selfish, since it's most of all to try to see it clearly myself. You know the seductive and slightly peculiar surroundings in which I live here, without work for the past six months. The portrait of Baroness Fanny I've painted for you would be a good likeness, I assure you, except that when one speaks of her it is always too simple. Now something truly fantastic is happening. Thinking about it upsets me unbearably and I have difficulty writing to you about it. Pierre Indemini is here, in Vienna. I am seeing him again. Pierre Indemini is Fanny's lover. I have discovered that the lover I used to hear her talk about so mysteriously was Pierre.

I do not have the resources to confront this fact.

What makes me suffer most is the following: how could I have come and placed myself here where this thing is happening? I beg you, tell me, my good Marguerite: perhaps you will be able to enlighten me?

I now see Pierre Indemini. He has touched me with a certain *demand* that he has made of me. I remain Fanny's friend, but I no longer have the least idea what ground we are walking on.

My letter is very confused.

Pierre Indemini does not seem to love Fanny. Compared to what he was before, he is a man of much greater prominence. My position is very false. Have I told you that Baroness Fanny had for a time displayed amorous feelings toward me?

Another letter:

You're right but I'm not wrong. Moreover, things develop from day to day. It isn't the lack of money that really stops me. I am *caught* here. I discover nothing. I do nothing. I am motionless and I hurt a little.

I meet Pierre outside, at the café. Our relations have gone back to being sweet and candid. We talk, but Fanny's name does not pass between us; it's an understanding. Thus, I can't hope that the current imbroglio between him and me will resolve itself; it's as if we are embarking on a new acquaintanceship. But in fact, didn't I *dream* that I surprised him in her apartment? It seems like it. I know that their relations are continuing. Pierre is not a hypocrite. Then what is the solution to this wretched situation?

Oh, if only I weren't so sluggish.

Felicitas is much stronger that I imagine.

Felicitas is looking wonderful. There is nothing for her but interest and pleasure in life. You should see her serving her "charming dinners" in the garden, in the evening, with her old table service on an enameled table.

She radiates life and optimism. Her husband and her son seem to be in love with her, or in any case they are absolutely proud of her. She declares that she will follow her son Guido to the ends of the earth, as long as he wants her . . .

The tenderness with which she surrounds me is more *tangible* than that sort of attachment we had come to before I discovered the truth. Should I say she is tormenting her soul? That would be using a big word . . . Or else a new mixture is being prepared in this way and I am afraid to think, without even conceiving of it clearly, what that could be.

She gives me all sorts of presents. Not a day goes by that I don't receive flowers, a pretty dress, a piece of jewelry (she gave me a very handsome ring, pearl and platinum, that I had happened to look at; if only you could see it on my little finger, Marguerite), or a white coat, continual acts of kindness; she has very refined taste and she knows what I like. I am worried. I ask you once again, why doesn't this disgust me?

"You ask me," said a final letter, "how I see myself. As very nasty. I think I'm brushing up against diabolical uglinesses, that I can make them out in the background, knowingly, but that I stay here to see, to see where this will go. Am I here to be a voyeur, or a martyr? Pierre and she don't love each other anymore, I'm sure of it. Right now she is 'working on' me, but, you know, in depth. I would like to make them suffer and I would like them to make me suffer. Pierre claims to be renewing his 'feelings' for me, but it is a lie since he is still f—ing her. As for her, she would like to bring me into a combination, a trio. No doubt she, too, wants to see someone else suffer, wants to see the person she loves most in the world suffer. I had a dream about her: she was doing gymnastics to please me and her naked arm began to swell, and swell, and it became a fairy-tale animal, very white and perfectly beautiful, that said to me, smiling, 'Now you can leave Vienna.' Would you like to ask your friend M . . . to explain this dream to me? No, my suggestion is stupid, dear Marguerite, don't say anything to M . . . But I'm feeling very anguished, Marguerite, because of everything: what I know, and what I don't know. You remember that two people have killed themselves for this woman. There's a Spanish proverb that says: the worst is always certain."

XXXV

Catherine and Pierre would walk through the streets of the inner city, usually without talking. Summer softened the stones but wasn't for them. Like two birds from a foreign place, their eyes were vague; even two birds of torment, foreign to the rest and astray in themselves. They moved in step. For they were the same size. For they were outside in order to be together. They were not essentially *together* except when they were silent. As in the beginning of their relationship in the old days, long silences prevailed.

They could not (and did not want to) emerge from them.

Each allowed the aspect of him- or herself most worthy of being loved to wander about aimlessly, escorted by memories, experiences, and the feeling of "nevermore."

They pursued nothing at all.

It also happened that each one would sneak a look at him- or herself in the mirror that the other held out, and they would not recognize themselves. "Have I changed so much?" However, they both remade themselves, though they did not know how: for dissension or for harmony?

If Catherine saw Pierre step back for her because the sidewalk was so narrow, she thought of that man who first captured her, "who captured her, let her go, and who would not capture her again"; and as for him, if he contemplated her from the corner of his eye, he knew that in a profounder reality they had never left each other. This did not mean that he had not betrayed her many times, that he had not gone elsewhere, that he would not betray her again—tomorrow, right away, always.

Their two silences made one. For words are said and understood, and stop there; but silence spreads, meets the other, and surrounds him and clasps him with a subterranean and fatal power. Pierre knew in this way that Catherine had driven him from her heart—without quite succeeding, it is true—while he himself had had the naïveté to keep her buried while hoping always to resuscitate her.

And that day, joining their two courages, they had at last said a few words "about life in the rue Jacob." They had not been able to restrain themselves from laughing over their incredible awkwardness in the old days (now that drama, real drama, was surrounding them here). They understood that they were once again becoming precious to each other. But they took good care not to examine it too clearly, to harden it, and above all to give the attachment a new meaning, a meaning that would be, how should one put it, how should one put it, loving?

"Actually now, how old are you?" said Catherine absently, "Thirty-three years old, or thirty-four? I'm over thirty-five! That's already so much."

In order to break a painful tension and, really, to live, their hands met. Then they held each other chastely by the fingertips for a long time and walked that way.

Near Grinzing, to which he had brought her back: "See you later?" said Pierre; and Catherine answered, "See you later," in a completely toneless voice.

XXXVI

Felicitas is talking to Catherine, and first off she says:

"Pierre Indemini is an astonishing boy, with a *rare* quality, of an *exceptional* value, but so weak and so sensual that I can understand very well that one might become disgusted by him.

"It's very true, what the poet said, that 'sensuality is the sea in which all our virtues are lost.'

"If I believe what I hear people say, there are supposedly two Pierres. One is the one we know. The other is a young scholar with an 'inspired' intelligence. I don't understand anything about genius. I'm an ignorant woman. But I know what a man is; and in everything I've seen of him I haven't discovered any genius. And you? Have you encountered it?

"You know? It is very hard for me to forgive him now for the harm he did you.

"Have you noticed how great is his fear of death? About this I really wish someone would enlighten me. Why is this man afraid of death? Tell me your opinion.

"Death is the lot of all of us—as late as possible! Pierre Indemini is vigorous and marvelously healthy. He can even be radiant.

Should youth think about death? Never. Youth is the creature that denies change. The idea of youth is absolute. In order not to die one has only to remain in the idea of perfect youth. The moment is eternal—the moment! And if you oppose progress, evolution, and aging, you remain in youth, that is, in being. That's what I say to Pierre Indemini, but he doesn't believe me when I talk to him (he's a Frenchman). Only the act consoles him. Isn't that so?

"His mind, which is so afraid, has invented a system, and I am sure he believes in an afterlife. As for me, on the contrary, what do I know? But I believe in life. He wants to run away from life. Then why be afraid of death, I say to him."

(Felicitas seemed perfectly satisfied with her reasoning.)

"Death will come and it will put us to sleep gently, gently, and we will become grass, roses, or some other creation of love. I love, I live in the intimate folds of love, and I am completely penetrated by its beauty; in the end I will stop loving, and I will die, I will sleep. Love, death, there is nothing more, and no doubt they are the same thing. If I have loved a great deal I will die well. Why torture myself? God will not deny me forgiveness. Pierre Indemini does not want to accept this view of the world. I fear he is very much an egotist and a coward with respect to life. His metaphysics and his biology are of no use to him. I assure you, it would be better not to think at all and to be like me, a poor woman, a creature of instinct. I feel very sorry for him. In his heart of hearts, he is still overwhelmed by sin.

"You have learned that one can never satisfy his expectation. He remains discontented. Life never warms him enough. It is true that his mind has a great *logical* force, but really, in such a case, the little eye of a woman is needed to perceive the lack of moral intelligence hidden underneath! I like Pierre very much. I owe him some noble and beautiful years. But I have the feeling that he is definitely moving away from me and that I am ceasing to be effective."

Almost at the same time, Fanny Felicitas proposed to Catherine that she come "with her to the pied-à-terre."

"No."

"You're right," she answered immediately. "I wanted to test you, and I expected you to refuse."

But Felicitas had not finished talking about "the heart of things."

"There are three of us, the famous three. The number three carries unhappiness in love.

"Each of the three loves himself or herself first of all. Then each is attracted to the new one, the third, without wanting to lose the second, but preventing the second and the third from coming together. There is a revolving jealousy.

"These complicated sufferings should be burned away within a single pleasure. But I am the only one to see this. Meanwhile, we are unhappy. What will become of our life?

"How long have you been in Vienna? In my house? Oh, I know you are working on 'your personality' and I'm not worried, one day you will fly away from here! But really, there are some little young ladies worth nothing at all who are taking the place of Catharina, foremost actress in French cinema, and then you will not be able to make them leave. . . . How amusing your real name is: Catherine Crachat, you ought to have used it on the screen also; it is really too amusing. . . . Almost a year that you have lived in my house and I am so happy about it. Yet I ask myself: *am I not causing your unhappiness?* I oughtn't to become attached to anyone. My heart is full of tyranny. I have become insanely attached to you, but also, naturally, I have scruples."

Catherine wrote to Marguerite de Douxmaison:

She is hurting me now.

I ask myself why she has begun doing this. True enough, I am refusing her threesome.

But I saw that she was enchanted by my refusal; then these must be the new ploys of her infernal love. And I am so disturbed, so cowardly, so stupefied, that I tolerate and will tolerate much more still. So does this mean she has me? Or that *I love her—him, I mean?* But I am hardly jealous at all, their meetings don't bother me if I have mine.

Imagine the most absurd thing imaginable, and you will have the state of my heart: I feel that she was a support for me until the past few days. She supported me so that I could endure Pierre, because I have such need of love and I am weak, weak . . . in Pierre's presence, and we were both of us, together, "Pierre's women" . . . I feel a profound distress at the idea of having to leave Ruh-Land driven out by animosity . . . Marguerite—I have to ask myself whom I love. And wretched as I am, Pierre must be saved, Pierre must be saved. What do I really want, then? Is it to have Pierre again completely? Alone for myself alone?

Marguerite, your poor sick friend,
Catherine
P.S. Come get me.
No, not yet.

XXXVII

Oh, that Pierre, let us resume our dueling with him. Why is he always a disappointment to my heart? Pierre the unknown. Pierre the impalpable. "In his personal sense." An egotist, said Felicitas (and Felicitas understands egotists, males).

Doesn't he see Catherine with the wound inside her? Won't he find anything? Catherine succeeded in talking to him about Felicitas, and after several thrusts and parries:

"Then you don't feel her *evil spell* against you?"

"What evil spell?"

"I feel it."

Catherine went on: "What goal is she pursuing?"

"What goal can one pursue?"

"Your . . . death."

She has said it, but once it is said—it is only a romantic idea. They look at each other. They know that the idea, as idea, is true. Pierre sneered.

"Thank you, Catherine. I know what she can do, and can't do." He appeared to have extreme contempt for Felicitas.

"You are her prisoner!"

"I certainly hope not. Felicitas is a demon from the cellar, a nice monster of nature. All this interests me to the highest degree. I may say that I've read with great profit the novel Felicitas."

"But," cried Catherine finally, "what about me!"

"Ah, yes, you—what about you."

He was at the window; all that could be seen of him was his silhouette.

XXXVIII

She packed her bags the first time without believing in it. But she took care of everything very well, so that it would be impossible, after that, for her not to leave. In this way, because of her meticulous care, she actually began to leave.

Thus, when we are in a rage, we hurl an object that is very dear to us onto the floor with a vague awareness of what may happen; and it breaks.

After her first effort she was lying stretched out on her bed, her eyes wide open, when she heard something white land on the floor. It was a letter, through the window, weighted with a little pebble; a letter from Pierre; thrown from the street? She rushed over to search with her eyes: outside, no one. It could also have come from Fanny's terrace, situated higher up and overlooking her window. It didn't matter! Back on her bed, she read:

> Dear mysterious woman,
> I think you don't see the nature of our new attachment. You don't

see it yet. However, now you are going to see it. I probably shouldn't urge the well to gush forth. But you are suffering. The singing bird has hollow eyes, he is blind. I am obliged to say to you at least:

I know where we are going.

I want to communicate to you the confidence I feel, which increases every day as the experience is revealed and develops: for the experience of Catherine's heart is pursued along very deep paths. What can they know, those who are watching you on the screen of the present story here in Vienna, what can they know of you, Catherine? Since they are ignorant of your mystic birth. It is precisely this that I wanted to remind you of, at the moment when I believe I feel for you *enough love,* and am at last capable of saying to you: I know where we are going.

XXXIX

She was reading the end over and over again, upset, starting from "the confidence I feel."

. . . When a prolonged whistle echoed through the garden. What did she see? Guido, his expression triumphant. Hey, her letter? It was he who had thrown it so well.

But someone was knocking at the door. Catherine hid her letter, and Felicitas came in.

"*My dear,* I'm taking you out tonight. You must put on the beautiful dress, the one I like best."

Catherine signaled no. Too much of a headache.

"Absolutely, my dear!" (It was Fanny's latest manner, very mysterious, childish, a touch of vulgarity enhancing it like a dash of red pepper in a tasteless dish.) "I want you to."

"No, I won't." Catherine shook her head back and forth, also childish. She had such need for silence, for tears. Fanny was so excited that she saw neither Pierre's envelope, left on the table, nor the open suitcase and the preparations for departure.

"*Figarohochzeit* will be superb this evening! We're going to the

Redoutensaal, and we are going to meet Pierre there."

"Together?"

"Together."

"No."

Her voice expires in her mouth.

"*The Marriage of Figaro,* my dear! And you don't yet know the Redoutensaal. It's magnificent. The old imperial ballroom. I danced there in the time of the Court. It's unforgettable."

"Herr von Sonnenfels?"

"Yes, of course, you haven't forgotten either."

"I'm not going. It means nothing to me."

"What a way to be talking to me, dear one, unkind one."

"Nothing of the sort. Leave me alone."

"But I haven't done anything bad, and so we shall both be with Pierre?"

"Pierre is all for it."

"Yes, of course."

"Enough, leave me alone! I'm not going!"

Fanny then noticed the suitcase and the objects arranged inside it; cruelty spread over her face.

"Here's the ticket, Catherine. *We* will be waiting for you in our seats."

Catherine read:

Redoutensaal		
Parkett	I	Kategorie
8 Reihe	Rechts Sitz Nr.	**72**
Dienstag, 17 Oktober		

"No, for the last time. Never."

Catherine pushed the ticket away from her on the table.

"As you like." Felicitas calmly picked up the ticket again, and along with the ticket *the envelope from Pierre's letter,* and thrust both into her bag.

"You understand almost nothing about life, Catharina, you are a Frenchwoman. In any case, put away the suitcase, because you're not close to leaving."

The ballroom is a rectangle occupied by the crowd, the general impression there is one of wealth and light; the white walls have gold inlay everywhere, the majestic, rounded vault contains a population of chandeliers; the style is beyond reproach. In the cloakroom, the women diffuse a natural smell of musk and gently comb their hair. Voices chatter. Let us go into the hall. The dances in the old days turned here at a ceremonial pace: the birthplace of the waltz. The orchestra is discreetly tuning up. Lifting one's head, one suspects that present in the remote corners are the shadows of cornices and the phantoms of crinolines. All the spectators have entered. The door opens one last time: to let Catherine in. Darkness descends, the adventure begins.

She has come. Alone, paying for her seat. She is placed where she belongs. Among the most ordinary red seats at the side.

They are listening to Mozart's music. Never had Catherine been more intensely transported; on the other hand, Catherine is independent. She is searching. One Catherine, in the kingdom of sounds, cries and laughs; the second Catherine lets her eyes rove. Before her extends the whole parterre, dimly lit. Where is that first category? It's quite far off. She searches, she rummages about, she stirs. Her gaze fixes upon heads, and immediately rejects them. Not him. Nor her. She is going to see *them.* At last see them together. Rejoined. Joined. Glued. She is going to know that they are truly two and one. She is going to martyr herself to this sight. She is going to surprise them without their clothes on. She is going to verify that the devil is there.

Catherine passes the rows in review. At the far ends of the hall is a vague humanity that frightens her. She begins again. She gets lost. Parquet 1st category. One line ended, she seizes another. There are also the people whom one sees from the back. Catherine tries to remember Felicitas's dress, but the design of that dress escapes her. Catherine soon enters into a diabolical character, who corresponds to the devil of the two others, and takes a somber pleasure in it. She has a daydream, during which she sees herself as a girl in a house in Paris, wiping white stains from her skin. Catherine, who is listening to the heaven of the music, the Countess's harrowing recitative, absolutely ignores all of these nightmares.

She is definitely not finding what she is looking for; she will never find it. There they are! She has them! They are here. Her joy chokes her. Pierre, very handsome, has his face turned to listen, leaning toward Felicitas. They are sitting in complete safety next to each other. The music makes them gentle and brilliant. They have the look—unreal, not alive—of an audience reflecting the action of a theater. They are pretty and clean. Happy. Rich. A strange and delicious scene is being enacted in them. Under Catherine's frantic gaze they do not tremble. Catherine feels that her life is lost because of those two, but not even the slightest shadow passes over them. All the same, they have been recognized! As she sees them? Felicitas must be holding Pierre's hand in secret, under a fold of her dress. How awful! Puritan Catherine imagines that she will have to be witness to the rest! She is sure that afterward they will go to the pied-à-terre. They will force her to watch. Everything; she knows the thing by heart. And what a reflection on herself! Catherine already faded, Felicitas youthful; Catherine frigid, and Felicitas the "great lover." Catherine is nasty, not a woman woman, a boy woman, a great street urchin. Catherine is a failed woman, a failed destiny, a failed artist in an ignoble, failed art. "And what about his letter? Why did he send me his letter? But I am Catherine Crachat! What if I were to kill both of them?" Catherine has a revolver, she walks ten paces, she fires at the woman's head. Bang! That Fanny falls, collapses like a rag, one less piece of filth on the earth! The hall breaks out in cries, the performance is stopped short, she is arrested. . . .

Nothing of the sort happens.

Oh, let me die. Oh, let me die.

XL

A miracle was occurring. Catherine was in a large unfamiliar room above the city, face to face with Pierre Indemini.

This is his new apartment, I think. A pale sun shone clearly, with hope.

The wind was brushing against the window.

Catherine, near that window, in which distant landscapes are crudely outlined, has her hair surrounded with a nimbus, and she is listening. She is listening because a great thing is going to come rushing up.

Catherine is wearing a very open white wool dress that ends at the knee, as is the fashion. Why has she appeared in this whiteness? Because he wrote to her: come with a white dress. Could she have not obeyed? But she is bothered by the opening of the dress.

Pierre, his back to the light, was paying no attention either to the dress or to Catherine. What is he thinking? He is not looking at her hair, sparkling with light. A newspaper is lying there. He says, "Doesn't the general strike they're announcing frighten you?" Catherine shrugs her shoulders and answers, "Let them blow the city up!"

The external event was not real in their eyes because the event in their consciousness was swiftly approaching. Depending on the colors of that event and the degrees of its success, they would be either alive or dead that evening.

"He loves me." Thus, groping, in a hoarse tone, spoke Catherine's private demon, her opaque being, who is she and whom she can no longer control.

"She loves me," Pierre Indemini said to himself in clear language.

"Catherine Crachat."

First he says her frightful name, name of bleeding and of pain. He says it several times, religiously. He spoke at a very great distance from her. He was looking at a blank wall.

"Catherine Crachat."

His face was certainly not his ordinary face; but a very serious, very beautiful idea like a furrow twisted it crosswise.

Thus from the ashes, from an incredible accumulation of ashes that they had formed together, the phoenix reemerges. The marvelous bird of love is formed anew. Love returns. Love wounds and weakens all resistance. Love causes excessive pains to be forgotten. But what a marvelously beautiful love once again.

We immediately abandon the earlier macerations, the blows struck at us, the misunderstandings, the divisions. We abandon the bad judgments, we abandon the distress.

He loves me. I love him. She loves me.

And now we receive the greatest blows that can be endured; with delight.

"Is it true, oh Catherine, that a single person was my love and has given it back to me?"

"I, Pierre."

"Is it true that you are the *only one?*"

"I believe it, Pierre."

"Is it true that only one has given me not mere pleasure but the gift of heaven?"

"I want that to be true, Pierre."

"And that there is only one soul to which I lay claim and one breath with which I have wished to identify myself?"

"I want that, Pierre."

"The creature for whom I reserve my veneration is you, Catherine."

"Yes, Pierre."

"The creature who takes me and who abandons me, who fulfills me and transfigures me."

"I hear it at last, Pierre."

She adds, "I am not speaking, I am answering; I am effusion."

"You don't have to speak today."

"Why, Pierre?"

"What you are goes so infinitely far beyond what I am. But I have a passion to reach you."

"   . . .   "

"I have a passion for your salvation and mine."

"   . . .   "

"I have an infinite ambition for the two of us. I want—a great deal."

Catherine wipes away her tears.

"I forgive you," she says.

Indeed, he wanted to hear those words.

A little later he explained to her: "Beautiful as you are, you contain a demon of a particular species. You have contained it since your birth. I love your demon. It is a demon of debauchery, of pain, and of chastity. O woman worthy of being loved. The demon itself is even pure. O fortunate one, hurled forward so pitilessly! And those great wild shining eyes and that neat mouth and those powerful bones under that face! Thus have I often seen you like the infernal Diana who presides over enchantments. She is not gentle. She does not have the light of day.

"It is not enough, o Catherine. In you, in your center, is the spark of another light. The spark of the opposite fire. I will name it charity. I will awaken it. I am already awakening it. In this reawakening or this awakening I will at last save myself."

She said, "Explain it to me more clearly."

"Our love will be bigger than we are. Our love will be *renunciation*."

"What?"

"Our love, in order to exist, must not make love one more time."

"I understand you."

"In Catherine's heart the same severe law strains to be realized. Isn't that true?"

"Yes."

"I received the warning of it inwardly. With that look of anguish you ask me why? You are afraid? I can't give reasons. It's necessary and I am trying . . . or *I am seeing*."

"Yes, Pierre."

Then he clasped Catherine in his arms, and over her he said that they were *one starting from this second*. That they would communicate to each other the substance of all the days of their lives. That they would live only for each other. That, each through the other, and with the help of the other, they would prepare for death. That there would no longer be in them any limit, any private wall, but everything unique, and since everything would also be renounced, everything would be purified. This was why they were going to leave each other this very day, in the full force of their adoration, and never see each other again.

Catherine moaned horribly, "I can't."

And then, "Have pity, Pierre . . . "

He laid his hand broadly on the pearly skin of Catherine's back, feeling it one last time, and without trembling.

Catherine lifted her head; she saw before her on the wall a watercolor entitled *Happy Day.*

A naked genie with long legs, a hard torso, a head covered with golden hair, with blue eyes. He is extending his arms, and at the end of his arms his hands are spread, as wide as possible. His face is serious, his gaze rather melancholy; his male sex innocent and strong. His feet, very far apart, for his legs are open, press on the ground like a dark lava. Day is breaking! Like a shell of rays, behind him the sky is rent; the sky is breaking open through the very head of the genie! Between the gloomy earth and this sky like an ejaculation, which the genie holds together, there is blackness: it is death.

Pierre Indemini says to Catherine, "In this way we will be together."

I GOT A TREE FROM THE
GARDEN OF LOVE ROOTED DEEP, DEEP IN MY
HEART . . .

XLI

In order to cut herself off from Ruh-Land *where she really had to be,* she stayed in her bed for a few days. Emptiness gently grew around her. Life moved away. Life for pleasure was over.

They knew she was not sick, but occupied with reflecting on the conditions of her being. They left her alone.

"Pierre loves me" and "I have to leave" were the two primary terms of her thinking. She abandoned them right away; she lost them on purpose, to plunge into curious, infinite fits of childishness, fantasies of figures, of memory. What a life, from one end to the other under the sign of privation. She was shaken by tremors, as in a fever. "Well, yes! Well, yes! With joy!" *For all Joy longs for Eternity—deep, deep Eternity.*

Catherine was looking for money.

She had no resources. One could measure the state of neglect into which she had allowed herself to fall. One could see that for a year she had lived off Fanny. By now it was impossible to make out the nature of her relations with Fanny. With an air of affectation, the baroness came to see how she was. Catherine did not know if a break, or what sort of a break, had occurred between Pierre and Fanny, but the thing was bound to happen, she felt it with absolute confidence.

Catherine needed money

There is a horrible marriage between the problems of your fate and the money you have in your purse. This money, the measure of your compromises and the total amount of your cleverness— is this what commands your mind and your heart? Without money, you stay here, motionless in the face of Felicitas's mounting hatred. Without money you do not carry out Pierre's superhuman plan for your new love, and your calvary does not come to pass . . .

And so she sent letters off in all directions, trying to get an engagement. "Give me whatever you like. I'll even work as an extra. Send a cash advance to this address . . . "

She counted on her fingers the number of days for the different answers. She calculated her chances. "Miraflor will apply to Lharb. Star-Film is producing a lot. Paramount won't answer."

There is also no relation between the problem of subsisting in the mystical path, loving while renouncing the promised joy— and those coarse events people are talking about. Vienna is in the midst of insurrection. Riots are taking place in the center of the city and the suburbs are cordoned off. The furious animosity against the workers that Felicitas immediately gives vent to is indicative of the current social ugliness.

One evening Baron Hohenstein was brought back to Ruh-Land slightly injured. He had been attacked and knocked around in the offices of his newspaper. But the principal emotion, the only emotion, of which Catherine was capable, came to her from an event that could not have as much meaning for anyone else as it did for her.

She was informed that the crowd had made its way into the Burg and was setting fires: *the Redoutensaal is in flames.*

"I knew it, I knew it would burn down!" She also thought: Now I am a little purer. And she went off on foot carrying her letter to Pierre.

XLII

Order was restored, Catherine had had no replies. In Paris they had forgotten her.

Catherine was to have left and was not leaving. Catherine needed money desperately.

How could she speak about this shame in her letters to Pierre? Instead, she said to him, "Allow me for just a few more days to go on breathing the same air as you." Two or three hundred schillings to get back to Paris by third class! The material problem absorbed her completely and the force of the difficulty anesthetized her heart.

Henceforth it was in Paris that she would find Pierre again. That she would carry out her promise, or kill herself. Two or three hundred schillings.

Guido! How was it she had not thought of it before? Guido, the only sincere friend she had in that house. He had probably begged her to let him be something for her, and she had turned a deaf ear. All the more reason. She could ask Guido.

She met him by the front gate, because he liked to emerge from a clump of trees in the garden and open the gate for her himself without waiting for someone inside the house to press the electric button. She said to him without preamble: "I need two hundred schillings to leave, Guido, and I am quite unhappy, would you lend it to me?" She must have looked so distraught that Guido forgot to kiss her hand as he usually did, but instead blushed and said, "Tomorrow, Mademoiselle Catherine!" thrusting his hands in his pockets.

And it was the evening of her birthday (thirty-six years old). She was in the drawing room, in Baroness Fanny Felicitas Hohenstein's museum, in Fanny's presence, separated from Fanny by a thick bouquet of flowers which the baroness had given her.

By general agreement the same people had come together in a group. They were waiting for Catherine to announce her imminent departure; and indeed she announced it on the evening of her birthday. (Will Guido find the money?) Thanking them infinitely for everything. To Felicitas, in particular, Catherine declared (feelings too mixed to be feigned) that she would never forget either her, or Ruh-Land, or Vienna, or . . . anything.

Guido vanished first. M. Hohenstein, who seemed affected by Catherine's departure, a little later.

Fanny Felicitas opened a cupboard from Venice with a hundred little drawers, and from the most secret she drew a folded paper, which she held out to Catherine. Catherine saw: a check, two hundred schillings, for Mademoiselle Catherine Crachat.

My God!

"The day before yesterday you chose to ask—Guido—for the sum . . . " (Fanny's voice rose by degrees to reach a tone of unhappy demand) " . . . the sum of two hundred schillings. I'm giving it to you. Happily, my son has no secrets from me. He betrayed you right away, my dear friend! I will say no more about it, it pains my heart too much, and . . . "

"I did no harm to Guido!"

"Excuse me. Excuse me. That is for me to judge. For me alone, do you understand?"

The check was on the tip of Catherine's bare hand. Had she taken it, then? Baroness Fanny was no longer looking at that hand.

"Isn't that so!" continued the baroness, furious. "Me! Because *to me* you did harm in my son. Isn't that so."

"To *you* I could not explain myself. I have run out of solutions. I thought that Guido was a man. I was wrong."

"Guido is *not* a man! Guido is mine!"

She was going much too far, and with that cunning mastery with which Catherine was familiar, Felicitas brought herself back to the correct position.

"You *ought* to have talked to me about it. Have I then behaved so very reprehensibly?"

"Ask you? Never."

"Allow me to differ entirely from your opinion as to the role which you wished to make my son play! And I will take good care, abiding by our friendship, not to reveal all my thoughts, for they might present some thorny sides for you! But since I was preparing this money I was clearly obliged, begging your pardon, to inform him about what happened at Ruh-Land this summer!"

"Inform him . . . about what happened . . . "

"Between you and me. I was obliged. I told him."

"What? You told him what?"

"Excuse me. Excuse me. My son is old enough to learn what happens to his mother. The good and the bad. My private life is known to him. It is my pride that I have such straightforward relations with my son. I am not afraid of embarrassing questions. Why shouldn't I tell him that you had hoped to inspire me with amorous feelings and that you were disappointed?"

Felicitas's glance sparkled with a sweet rage.

As for Catherine, she felt emerging miraculously inside her the strength to withstand such insult. She was overcome by a feeling of calm.

"Good-bye, Felicitas, you have lied."

"Lied? Would it be I, by some chance, who ran after you? Or you who spied on me until you discovered my affair, and spoke to my lover? Didn't I furnish *the proof* to Guido when I told him that we loved the same man and that this did not stop you from continuing to live in my house?"

XLIII

Catherine Crachat left Ruh-Land at eight-thirty the next morning. She saw Guido in the front hall. He was pacing up and down there. In a very bad mood. And she said to him, "Good-bye, Guido"; he answered, "Good-bye, Mademoiselle Catherine," in a tone so earnest and so humble that she stopped. She looked him in the eyes. "I don't hold anything against you, Guido." He, being about to give way to tears, hunched his shoulders.

Guido looked toward his mother's room. Catherine said, "Yes, yes!" so that he would feel calmer. However, since she had been humiliated in the boy's heart: "You must be skeptical like Saint Thomas, and believe only, good as well as bad, what you have touched with your own finger."

Guido called his great dane, which he had brought in with him. "Pet my dog?" and he added, "in remembrance?"

Guido hurried to open the gate of the house for her one last time. They were carrying out Catherine's suitcases. The cook, weeping, was saying, "*Bitte kommt wieder!*" On the second floor, on the terrace, leaning on her son's arm, was Fanny Felicitas. She gestured affectionately to the traveler with her hand.

Catherine, who had torn up the check in front of Fanny the night before, had enough in her purse to have herself driven to the Hotel Regina. There she sent a telegram (please put it on the bill) to Marguerite de Douxmaison, and through the doorman she notified Pierre Indemini. Pierre telephoned at noon. He wanted to see her again.

She spent half an hour at his apartment in the evening, and it was extraordinary for her and for him; the Promise was kept.

The next day the money was there: Flore Migett sent five thousand francs. Everything was becoming as simple as ABC. Also the next day, two letters from Pierre on her table. She was radiant. Catherine was to leave Vienna that afternoon.

To leave—because love wants everything—except to leave. Here she is in the city, she is taking another brief walk. All the threads of her presence here having already been broken, she had a dizzying access of despair: "to see Pierre one more time!"—followed by a desire for immediate death by any means at all. She stopped a car and gave Pierre's address. She opened the door of the moving vehicle . . . She looked at the pavement. She read on the pavement:

Catherine is losing her only love . . .
Catherine has debased herself with Felicitas . . .

Felicitas wants to kill Pierre . . .
Guido has been scandalized . . .
Felicitas hates Catherine . . .
Catherine is losing her only love.
Hatred, failure, and death.

She had the car turn in a different direction. They were passing in front of Saint Stefan's Cathedral. She got out. The interior of the basilica was violet, strange, and of a depth as though in close intimacy with death. Creatures in black were lost in prayer. She went through it like a madwoman.

She returned to the hotel, collected her suitcases since she was no longer detained by anyone, paid, found herself looking at the train. She stepped up into the train.

XLIV

. . . There are a lot of people in the rue Jacob, people waiting for her to arrive, to embrace her, to put her to work.

She is working.

She leads this life: religious with a secret love. But in this century, you understand, among men. What men.

She receives from Pierre Indemini her life—strictly speaking, her life—every morning. By sheer force of energy and creation she can continue as far as the next day at the hour when the mail comes. Pierre lives in the same way she does. She knows it.

In a second, "infra" life, she allows herself to open her eyes: this is her art, because everything in it belongs to a dream, is not real. During this period Catharina plays her greatest roles.

THE SPIRITUAL LIFE OF
CATHERINE CRACHAT

XLV

Brought back to her point of departure, Catherine Crachat entered upon a time of torture. In this place where I was vile for twenty years, vile and easy, I am undertaking the death of desires. I will never succeed in this, never, for I do not *want* to succeed in it, my desire being all my fire and all my good and all my recompense at last! But I want with another will to do *his* will, and his will whose sacred direction I feel in me wants the death of desires. And why not my death? But she saw herself terribly alive and not capable of suicide, unless it was to kill herself by impulse, accident. And then, I love him: I have no more rights over myself; I love him, I belong to him in eternity. This reason was very real: it was enough to evoke it, and all disturbance disappeared like those diabolical little apparitions of persons that she saw appear down on the ground and that she could drive off at will into the dark corners. Catherine persisted in living in order to love, and through loving to redeem love; for the love of a Crachat is to be redeemed, and love in general, too, moreover: it is so heavy, so dirty, and so demoniacal in the beginning; to love, and through the fact of loving without a caress of love, to transport to a higher place, more purely, farther into the heavens, one's heart. This was Pierre's idea. Catherine understood this idea of Pierre's very well and through love of this idea even strengthened her own love; but the opposite sometimes occurred, the idea strengthened her desire, the desire that is the natural product of the eyes, the mouth, the hands, the hips, the body; and then it was atrocious.

Catherine Crachat came and went, left the studio. She put on her fur, she shone like a star of night. She received people in her home and answered questions; then she took her clothes off without any light because she was afraid to see herself; now she was naked. She could not cover her nakedness and felt she was suffocating.

She for whom sex scarcely existed any longer . . .

Struggling with forces higher, darker than the clearest forces of her heart could gracefully and clearly fight, she recognized in these forces of the demon her own forces once again. She had not wanted to remove anything from them, to diminish them in any way, in order not to diminish the struggle; for the struggle is salvation, it is love of Pierre, it is Pierre's mouth speaking, it is the New Life.

Love drew from her deep tears, tears she had never felt on her cheeks, never tasted.

Then she fell asleep.

She lived off one letter a day.

She lived off reading the message "I love you" written in one handwriting or another. She was alert to everything. In addition, she was also certain she was communicating directly with him. Receiving his joys. Passing on to him her own, and her fears. Making, across the distance, the same motions he was.

I receive from Pierre my daily life. This day will produce nothing in our favor. This is because he and I receive our daily bread from a higher hand.

Through sheer force of creation I can go on until the next day at the hour the mail comes.

Pierre lives the way I live. I am absolutely sure of Pierre. Absolutely calm; absolutely tranquil. I am loved absolutely. I am an absolute lover.

She felt as though the distance, by removing from love its weight, its smell, the disturbance of the bodies, by removing from love the thorny difficulties of minds, but in wresting from it the will, in castrating it, had made two hearts abnormally naked, exposed, burning, forsaken in order to be pure, prepared to die on the path of perfection.

But that same night she would groan, smothering the words from her mouth in the pillow: I need . . . come back . . . —and then she would get up and she would break whatever happened to fall under her hand.

During the first months, the daylight went on darkening and then lightening out of all proportion and beyond all reason. Impossible to say how she would emerge from it.

Doubting everything, believing in everything, no one knew anything about what she was enduring. Only Pierre out of all the world.

Their letters did not merely have that intimacy of tone and that detail that turn a correspondence between lovers into an endless murmur in the ear. But because they were never going to see each other again they dared to say everything, and if the desire of their voices was to go up to heaven through an infinitely free movement that would have made them blush in each other's presence, they allowed themselves to go.

Pierre intoned the song.

Catherine answered.

Catherine sang first.

"But there was not a minute," Catherine will say later, "when I did not hear the sigh expressing the pain of what we were doing."

The day of the anniversary (one year since her departure from Vienna) she read:

> I am abandoning myself, I am abandoning myself and becoming supple in a spiritual exercise of departing, since it is necessary to leave. At present I ought to be able, thanks to the light you give, thanks to your *ladder* of light, to stare at the enormously formidable heavens with the tranquillity of Jacob.
>
> I make you (madly and without knowing it) my sister in eternal desire, in imperishable love. I am certain I will always find you again. If I survive, I cannot be without your breath. If a breath coming from

you exists, I cannot fail to survive.

In order to steer as best I can this strange ship of *new belief* I read the Church Fathers; above all the pure and moving Augustine. I am sending you the books with marks.

I also meditate on the words of Michel Le Tellier in his last hour: "I do not wish for an end to my sufferings, but I wish to see God."

I am writing poems.

I am full of *confidence*.

She did not pay enough attention to this sign.

In the course of the following summer the letters became a little less frequent. Very gradually, as though he did not want Catherine to notice it. One or two days passed.

Pierre Indemini was deep in a very exacting work, or else, indisposed, he was suffering from states of depression during which he did not want to write.

But everything was still the same between them.

They came to the beginning of winter. She was infinitely tired, harassed. She felt that some sort of event was occurring.

Run to him! (But lose what they had gained?) Go away again right after . . . But once, just one time . . .

. . . .

XLVI

From Saturday to Friday there were no letters. On Friday she telegraphed. No answer. On Saturday she sent another telegram, to Fanny Felicitas. I'm very aware that they have separated; but I can't believe she knows nothing about him.

On Sunday, nothing.

On Tuesday: "*Liebe* Catherine, my dear sister . . . "

A whirlwind of blackness went through her from her feet to her head, and she fainted.

Liebe Catherine, my dear sister.

I say my dear sister right away with all the force of my soul. I will perhaps be permitted to bring us together in this way at such a solemn time. But then I no longer wish to speak, only to cry. I am stifled by our unhappiness. Oh sister! Pierre Indemini is no longer. Pierre has left us both, has left our hearts, which loved him with such fidelity, to go into that world in the heavens which he had created and dreamed. And neither you nor I saw him go! Neither one of us was able to close his eyes.

I pray, I pray to God. This does not dry my tears.

He had left Vienna ten days before, ill. He had left suddenly.

Why this trip, why this flight?

I was no longer seeing him as I had before, of course. Therefore I was without influence. I only knew this: that his heart was no longer working very well. He always hid this from you.

When he went, he left me a note indicating his new address: Astano in Italy. I do not know the region. It is a village. Why not have gone to you, Catherine?

It was there in that place, Astano, when he had just barely arrived, that he left this life. I still can't believe it! I still can't believe it! I had seen him again once or twice this summer, he appeared to be in admirable health; only that heart of his . . . The people of Astano found his address in Vienna, and mine. They notified me. I did all that was necessary. What will have to be done now we will decide together.

He is sleeping there by the church.

Liebe Catherine!

The distress that fills my soul I can hardly describe to you who know everything about Fanny Felicitas Hohenstein. I bear a cross. But I feel the cross you bear too. I am afraid for your life, your health. Do you want me to come to Paris? We both loved one man, Pierre Indemini; then will you allow me to kiss your forehead? *Liebe* Catherine, just think that he ran off far away from me, ill, just think that he did not want me there at the end. Have pity on me. If he left me his address when he went, it was only because of you. I do not rebel. I perform with love the duty with which he entrusted me. But I am suffering. I am suffering because years of happiness are being reduced to nothing. No, this is not a selfish sorrow on my part; it is the pain of a child who did not know, who did not know how to love enough! But I want to respect your grief which has so much more motive than mine! What will I say in your presence? Perhaps grief is deranging me . . . It seems to me he no longer loved anyone—but himself! Forgive me once again, Catherine. Never will we be able to understand what has happened; and never will we be able to separate. Thus assures you

    Your faithful friend who loves you,

      Fanny Felicitas Hohenstein

P.S. I could arrive in Paris Wednesday.

Two days later Catherine, floating on the abyss, saw *a letter,* another letter, arrive at her bedside. Postmark: Astano (Ticino). Handwriting unfamiliar. The envelope opened to release a letter *from Pierre.*

    Dear Creature

    (what would I not give to see the features of your face again).

    You must not be worried nor sad nor revolted. You must not be afraid. You must not feel lost or dispossessed. You must not think of dying. You must remain gentle, impenetrable to misfortune. You must smile. You must remain beautiful but henceforth no longer be real for anyone. You belong to me. You must keep this secret with lips sealed and not open them in all your life except in the presence of the one who can understand. You are happy today. Because my feeling under the effect of yours has reached an incandescence so light that nothing, nothing in the hour to come appears difficult to me any longer.

    . . . I left that place because it was necessary. Here I am surrounded by the softest blue mountains there could be in our imagination.

    My fatigue made the trip difficult. I tolerated it well. Happily you were waiting for me here on the threshold of the door to the stone house, I saw you distinctly and you have not left me.

    For certain men all security of living is in relation to the morning. Here I feel I am always in the morning. You are here in the morning light, and before your amused eyes I parade plans for lives, works, that amaze even me. The morning here is of a dark brightness, it is so strong. The sky shows its depth. One understands Francis of Assisi as one had never before suspected. But I also show you the stars of the night. They are incredibly hard, palpitating and iridescent. You learn with me to *feel* the black space between the stars, that there is but the One substance and that in it everything is assured.

My room is small, painted pink. The chestnut trees will shade it in summer; the church overlooks it. A wooden bed and an old table. Another day I will talk to you about my work because here I am at the point where a man at last does what he wants to, after having been led for so long . . .

Interruption, and farther down, in a different handwriting:

If your heart has persuaded you to come, Catherine, no, you should not.

Thank you for having helped me in my salvation.

The letter also contained a second piece of paper with some Italian: *Io sono la moglie del proprietario della casa. Prima di morire, di morte dolce, il povero signore francese aveva raccomandato di spedire la lettera a Lei.*

Angela.

XLVII

Catherine Crachat Confesses

Pierre who is dying—oh, that has always been.

Everything comes together at a single stroke. What one has always been, one is. A part of oneself that one believed to be true is obliterated by grief. Another part appears—eternal, bleeding—which explains destiny because it *is* destiny.

"I am your desire of the father. I am you abandoned by your

father." Look at me carefully. I am your love. Your old first love.

Pierre Indemini appeared in order to save me. He must love me, he loves me, but he does not give me love; he exhausts me, he makes me bleed, and he dies.

Pierre dying was, for me who was opening my eyes wide, who was so pale, an expected, known event, it was a natural event, for me. *I knew it very well!* I listened to the mysterious allusions, I went down into my underground spaces. Pierre abandoning me through his cowardly death, oh that was inscribed in the inside of my flesh.

The little girl has a father. She can't name this father. She has no *right* to this father. The father is forbidden. She watches him go by behind a hedge, and he is a black form stooping forward. Then, in the same black way, Pierre is the new father whom she can't name. She suffers, she suffers inexhaustibly behind the hedge, at the idea of seeing the father and that she will be deprived of this father as long as she lives. Is he even the father? Yet she sees him. The father's head is bowed, the transgressing forbidden father. He goes by. He almost brushes against his daughter hidden by a hawthorn bush. The little girl grimaces with pain . . .

And also because the shock is produced upon *the death,* and because the death horrifies me and smothers me by covering Pierre, wonderful Pierre, with the smell of a cadaver—but also because that very peaceful death was present between us from the beginning and made us love each other more, so that the nightmare can almost pour out into the light; because a preparation of that death in spirit had been made by him, received by me; and because this absolute loss "without spirit of return" is his thought, what he wanted; and because he dies, so to speak, *as he loves me:* I feel—that having always been unhappy and deprived I will perhaps at last find the solution to the unhappiness and be able to do what Pierre Indemini asked. I will be loved and succeed in loving in the path that He desires. When I name him I apply to *Him* a divine capital letter. I was not able to do His will as long as he was alive. I was too much of a sexual animal. Now . . .

The rolling wave of grief came from so far away, from the source, and rose upon me, to the point that I no longer knew precisely whom I had lost, only that I had lost *everything*, the wave of grief, the only wave of grief that I could know, one single time, one single day, an eternal day, had taken possession of my being because it was at home there. And at the same time the motion of that wave, so destructive, bore one inanimate; almost dead; awakening one could glimpse, hope to go toward, drag oneself to the feet of deliverance, seek a place on which perhaps to set one's lips for the kiss of deliverance . . .

"So that my eyes appeared to have become two things that no longer wished for anything but to weep. And it happened that because these tears continued so long, my eyes were in the end rimmed by that redness which is the stigma of martyrizing thoughts."

. . . .

XLVIII

Story

I leave Paris to bury myself in the isolation of this little farmhouse where I am now. I make a permanent break. I am supported by several devoted friends. I have no further need of anything.

I am here for several months when there looms up before me a new test: I must see Felicitas again.

Why face the world yet once more? Already I felt like an invalid, a blind woman.

The main problem was that Pierre's body was in Astano and certain measures had to be taken there or it had to be brought back to France.

Something else had the greatest importance for me. Felicitas and I had written to each other. Spontaneously, in one of her last replies, she spoke of a packet of letters of Pierre's bearing the superscription "To my guide," which she happened to have. These letters, I did not doubt for a second, were for me and I wanted to recover them.

We decide to meet in an unfamiliar place in Bavaria.

I have the feeling that the letters are absolutely precious and will be revealing to me. I am going in order to get the letters back. A great weakness comes over me before this departure. It seems to me that I have already lost all touch with the world, and yet that I am abandoning my discipline.

Yes, yes, it was necessary that I seize every occasion to leave my "dream" in order to recapture, verify, a fragment of his life, reenter the real, with memory, echoes. It was necessary that I know as much as possible, that I even explain to myself at last Felicitas's presence in his destiny. And how could I admit that after two years there was a packet of letters I did not know about!

I was the first to arrive at Lake Eibsee in Bavaria. It is a black lake at an altitude of thirty-six hundred feet.

I entered a large cosmopolitan hotel which was altogether *isolated:* forests, water, not a peasant chalet nor a farm anywhere about. She chose her spot well.

No one passes by. One hears only an ax striking in the distance. A sleepwalker in this nature, I discovered the countryside at random. Here I felt that nature is a dark and stormy beast that wants to crush you, but will not crush you yet because you have in your heart a beast just like it. My long walks were distractions from my impatience, from my emotion. I would return to the hotel with the dismayed hope of finding her. No, not yet. I was like an owl at noon when the merciless swallows peck at its eyes.

He was always with me. I could not imagine that this air was not his air, that this ground was not his ground. I felt he was counseling me to wait and to be gentle, human in my manner of behaving. What did the bathers and the luxury of the hotel matter to us? *I was here for him.* While walking I had discovered in a secluded spot a cove with rocks awash, of a clear color, and delicate reeds against the sky, and blue; a very gay splashing formed around the dead trees; no one must come here but Him, led by me—never her, never Felicitas.

Fanny Felicitas arrived on a day of heavy rain. In the room where we were forced to remain, a false cordiality was established. We appeared affectionate; in reality we were trembling with fear. She had changed a great deal. I had changed even more for her.

At first sight, her desire had ceased, I mean her desire in general. She was living apart from Baron Hohenstein. I understood that the famous house was going to be sold. Her son Guido was in America.

I refused to talk about myself. But I saw that she was staring at me with astonishment. I was (she claimed) behind something thicker than a window, heavier than the depths of the water. I said nothing in reply.

She took care to confide to me that for the past three years her nights had most often been sleepless. This was our way of referring to Pierre Indemini. But I did not believe her.

No, I said to myself, he never knew this woman. It was quite insignificant to me that the shade of Pierre passed by, that the *name* was soon uttered by the mouth of this woman, and that her eye then looked at me in a furtive, cruel manner. Pierre the man, man of weakness and of pleasure, had enjoyed her. Pierre transcendent did not see her and did not know her. The vulgarity of the egotism I was observing stupefied me. Formerly it was embellished with the little flowers of poetry and religion, above all decked out in a lively tenderness; now it is coarse and trivial. I see she is attached to the crudest objects of egotism: her room, her bath, the menu, occupy half of her conversations. She besieges the hotel clerk, whom she calls familiarly by his name, Herr Triebe, with her demands. She talks readily about her intestinal ailments, about the cures advised, which she has tried, about the doctors she has seen, for she spends a part of the year in sanatoriums.

Death burns with its fire and purifies the creature that we are. It was when we came to the subject of *his death* that Felicitas and I could establish a state that approached harmony. Since nothing was any longer equal to what had been, we could think together what a favor we had received. And the fact that we were created to hate one another did not prevent the figure of Pierre from reconciling us through death.

But also because Pierre was our only "subject," our reason for being at Eibsee and for seeing each other one last time, the reality we could talk about without ever reaching the end and from which neither one of us would have been able to exclude the other, very often we walked forward for hours through woods dark and colorful (they were vast, truly sad) without opening our lips.

Soon I rediscover her, alas, I recognize her. She shows me a photograph of "Fanny Felicitas at twenty-four years of age," of which she is still very proud. She is naked, but the snapshot stops where it should. Arched, her head thrown back, with a thick mane of hair tumbling from it; her eyes closed; her hand under her breast in the area of her heart. And why show me this in the circumstances in which we find ourselves?

Why did I not understand then that in Felicitas nothing is yielded, nothing is transformed?

I still did not dare to broach the question of the letters. I was afraid of my anger if she refused them to me. When I understood that I was afraid, and afraid of myself, that drove me forward. The thing came through a sort of explosion, in the hotel stairway.

"Give me the letters that do not belong to you," I said.

She answered very much in control of herself, "But, dear, they are mine!"

"What do you mean—addressed to you?"

"I don't know. In my possession."

"The letters were written for me!"

She said with malice (I had no doubt turned pale), "Hold onto the bannister."

In her room, with the second padded door closed on the first, we were able to "go to it."

"The letters, Fanny. I want the letters."

"How impulsive you are. Why would the letters be yours, I ask you?"

"You possess a packet of letters sent back from Astano after his death, yes or no?"

"Certainly."

"On which he wrote: *To my guide.*"

"The guide isn't you, I wouldn't think."

"Or you?"

"Excuse me, I am much more modest, dear Catherine! Much more modest." (Her voice was wheezing and her eyes were full of tears.) "If I don't know *the person* to whom the letters are addressed, that is because the person—in my modest opinion—does not exist! These letters, like other reliquiae from his life, having come into my possession, I do not see why I should dispossess myself of what he left me."

I was ashamed of my anger. I said, "Forgive me, Felicitas, and show me the letters, would you?"

"I don't know if I should."

My anger resurged.

"You've read the letters?"

"Yes, of course."

"Well then, you have violated our secret, Pierre's and mine."

I was strangely confident, having only presumptions; as is a heart that lives off a faith in love when that faith is at stake.

"Give me my letters."

"What insolence you have," she said coldly. "One explains it to you, and it is of no use. Why do you want those letters so much? Because your love with him was created through letters?"

Her malice is bared in each feature of her face.

"Fanny, you admit that there is doubt about the person. You have read the letters. I have not read them. I ask to read the letters. When we agreed to see each other again, it was in order to read these letters."

"You are mistaken."

I shouted, "What sort of person is 'the guide' in the letters?"

"She's a woman, but from his imagination, a pure, poetical being: I don't know if you can understand this thing."

She was insulting me.

"Give me *my* letters"—I was exhausted.

As of that moment I had a horror of her. The phantoms who accompanied that woman reappeared: from the first lover who killed himself, to Elisabeth who killed herself, to Pierre.

I left her room that same instant. I did not want to take the letters, she should instead give them to me.

At dinner I joined a Felicitas who had changed yet again, rejuvenated, sugar and sweetness. Oh, what a Proteus, I thought; and the painful charm that comes from such a depth of despair began to have its effect again. She knew it and was in possession of all her means. She entreated me to forgive her.

I can guess where the letters are. Not in her room. She has handed over to the hotel desk, to that clerk named Triebe, a large man with small legs, a shaved head, and disgustingly polite—she has handed over to him a small yellow suitcase. It is the clerk Triebe who is keeping Pierre Indemini's most secret correspondence with the woman he loves.

Every day I think she is going to make up her mind to give me the letters. I am disappointed. Until the hour I take the letters in my hand, I feel myself in a situation of *duty* and at the same time of *mad desire* with regard to Pierre. For him I will endure anything.

Ten o'clock in the morning. I was in my room and was dressing. Probably the dead bolts of the doors could be opened from the outside with a master key that Triebe possessed. Baroness Fanny came in. I was more or less naked. Right away she looked at me as thoroughly as she could, from head to toe.

She was holding a cardboard box—a shoe box. When she decided to speak, she said, "Here they are." I was mute, motionless as marble. "I realize they belong to you. Here are *your* letters," she repeated.

The letters.

I held out my hand. She threw herself on my arm and kissed it furiously, voraciously. Her eyes blazing. I jumped behind the bed. I would have roused the hotel. All, all of the past loomed up again *and now I understood what purpose, in her mind, these letters were meant to serve.*

That same day I find myself with her by the water. Was I, then, going to give in to her, would I be weaker than she? I reexamined the curve of my life with an extraordinary lucidity and in an extraordinarily tragic light. I had locked the letters in my suitcase. I had the key to that suitcase, I was carrying it on me. Our whole story was reaching its term. Why was I still sitting next to her? Soon I analyzed the word *term;* I realized that it was wrong if it meant nothing more would happen; that on the contrary it was correct if it meant expiration, the end of one motion and the beginning of another, the moment agreed upon for settling accounts. What marked the term was the feeling that I was the object of her hatred and that she was the object of my hatred. Just as I felt the hardness of the ground under my feet, just as I saw the brightness of the setting sun red on the pine needles, so did I feel her hatred, the fluid of her mind speculating on my death and reflecting on the manner of achieving it. It no longer differed from the love for me with which she was once again smitten. This was the sense in which I was thinking: am I going to give in to her? Everything wanted a mortal struggle between us. Everything was leading us to fight. A duel. Blows. Who would break the other?

Each of us was musing on the role she wished to play.

The next day she suggested to me that we "go to the end of the lake along the shore and come back along the hilltops, crossing through the forest pass"—"four hours of walking with me?" I could only answer yes! As though that was just what I was expecting.

The path followed the water close to the rushes; on the rock the heat of the day was still like a wet cloth that one pushed aside in order to pass. She was in front. "Given her hatred, the forest, her physical strength, my spiritual will—and Pierre—should I defend myself or not?" I want to burst into tears, escape my headache, and run off as fast as I can. I do nothing of the kind. The fear of being a coward keeps me trailing at her heels.

At the far end of the lake, the twilight on the rocks, the slopes of mud, appeared sinister to us. We had already walked for two hours. We were calmer. Perhaps the nightmare was dissipating. Felicitas, turning her head, smiled at me. I, too, smiled. Then she rested her eyes on me openly and with lassitude, without trying to take an undue pleasure. We sat down on a rock and chatted in a natural way.

I placed about Fanny's shoulders a small shawl I was carrying in my hand, for fear she would catch cold, and we entered the deep forests in order to go back. We decided not to go through the pass.

In the forest we encountered the same heat as at the beginning of the walk. All of a sudden night swooped down on us. We were walking side by side now, the path was quite wide. Why did I still feel exposed? Was it indeed that at that moment I was beginning once again to wish she was dead? But I would not touch a hair on her head. That was settled. I went along, then, detached from everything; my destiny was playing with me. And I can still experience, listen to, Felicitas's soft, sad voice in my ear. She was talking about her son Guido. She was saying that "in the impure whirlwind of her life—only one worthy thing had existed, however paradoxical that might seem *on her part,* and that was her love for Guido. She had tyrannized him every day, it was true, and quite misunderstood him, treated him quite badly as a consequence . . . Guido was the pure dream of her life." I tried to look at her: she was all black, we were in the shadows.

"Guido will come back to you."

"Never. He will not come back. He will never come back."

She had talked to me, I think, about a fiancée in Vienna . . .

"But what about his fiancée?"

"She's not a real fiancée. He doesn't love her. He detests me. The fiancée is also me. Guido will never come back."

At the spot we had reached, we were supposed to find a path to the right toward the hotel, "marked with a sign." The forest was black as ink; a last glimmer of light at our feet.

I asked her, "Haven't you seen where the path is?"

"Certainly not."

I went on to say, "We absolutely must be on it before night falls completely!"

I felt unstrung by her response. Felicitas was not worried about the path.

The forest was of the blackest mold and went downhill. A thin crescent moon could be seen up above, surrounded by the hairy tips of the pines. Night had fallen. Noises of animals could be heard everywhere. It would pass over you, their wings. Things trembled, shadows walked with you. And that frightening Felicitas who knows that *we are lost* . . . and who simply follows me. All the submissiveness I had (after the setting of the sun) changes into fear, into nameless dread, into nervous tension. The most immediate and most intense forms of terror jostle against one another in my mind. Those which come to me from the darkness, from the animals, from the uneven ground, from hunger, from cold; those which are breathed at me by Felicitas and her hatred and the desire to murder that we had felt together . . . at the start of the walk.

I talk fast, "in order to talk us back onto the path." I resume a little control of myself. I talk to ward off dangers greater than I and greater than she. As for her, she remains silent. We go at random through broken branches, toward the right. Beyond any path, into holes. We hurt ourselves and utter muffled cries.

It was indeed I who first abandoned our course. We can't find it again. We give up on it. We do not see anything emerge: ghosts of trees, hollows in the ground. Fanny follows me like a dog. We seek comfort in the fact that "it's going downhill." All of a sudden we have to stop, out of breath, and her all but invisible white blouse is beating against mine. We touch: the sound of water.

There is going to be something horrible. We hear the sound of water. I glimpse her eyes: a spark of fury. I lunge some steps forward. I almost fall. She lifts me up. Her breast is heaving much more strongly and I feel the smell of her sweat like a cloud enveloping her. I am dizzy. I am dizzy because of me and because of her. The place and the moment. What hatred I feel. What hatred. We are still hesitating between contrary impulses. Wavering. Allow myself to be killed, love her or kill her . . . Who will go first, who will deal the blow, who will cut the knot? I hear her heavy panting, like the bellows of a forge. Me—or me? No, not me, *you!* She stood pressed against me, her fists closed; I wept, but like a demon. And, little by little (the monster unglues its mouth, its sucker, it releases you), I knew that I would not attack. Then go ahead! Let her go ahead then, let her be done with it! Come on, push me. "Well, go ahead then!" I said to her out loud. No vestige of charity left in my soul; I was saying good-bye to my life.

. . . No, she is still alive. *She cannot. I sneer.* She is changing completely, her hand moves a little (the revolver from the pocket of her skirt), applies it to herself, and right away it's over.

"Help! He-e-lp!"

The cry I utter comes out of my mouth with an extraordinary difficulty; I howl, I truly wrest it from my bowels. I can no longer see Felicitas. I flee from the spot, I try to return to it, now I can't find Felicitas . . . Everything is calm . . . Trees, real trees . . . I can begin to see them, quite real, dry reality, the earth . . . it is dawn. I don't know where, I was found unconscious by some bathers.

I was delivered.

That Fanny Felicitas had killed herself gave me no joy, no, but the satisfaction of an end. That is exactly what it was. At last. And to have seen her fall horrified me.

I realized that my prolonged unconsciousness had worked a transformation of my inner being. I had fallen a certain woman, I awoke another. In my faint I had plunged beneath my horror, and through the faint that marks the true depth of grief to the point of abolishing the sense of grief, I cut myself into two parts, into two people.

I did not ask myself any questions. Recumbent like a dying woman on a bed in Garm . . . where I had been transported, I moved a funereal lamp about inside myself but without illuminating any remorse. To have been delivered—that was my conviction, it left all else behind. No, I am not a saint.

"If thou knewest thy sins, thou wouldst lose heart."

XLIX

With Flore

A young woman entered. Not quite as tall as Catherine. Similar.

Their elongated forms as in an El Greco figure are almost identical. In particular, the same head of hair and the same complexion, only the cut of the hair is different, Catherine's forehead is uncovered and the other's is not. The same full oval for the face and the eyes underlined in the same way. This one has a smaller mouth than Catherine's, shoulders more closely set, heavier breasts, Catherine having broad shoulders, presently pure and almost thin.

There is a hardness in their faces.

Lastly, Catherine has a touching dark gaze; the second Catherine has brown eyes, velvet brown, which move as they correspond to the motion of Catherine's eyes. Like Catherine, she seems to aim for the heart of another person and to be immediately dismayed at what is going to ensue.

"You don't yet know Flore Migett very well. Here is Flore Migett."

And Catherine adds, "The companion of my days."

The physical resemblance of persons from the same family can startle us. What are we to say if, where no kinship exists, we observe bodies deciding to imitate each other?

Catherine Crachat and Flore Migett resemble each other like two sisters—more than two sisters, like two ideas of which Catherine Crachat would be the original. One must find these sorts of resemblances in cloisters. Their similarity is born of their spirits' acquiescence in the same truth. They are two creatures hungering for the same privation after having experienced the same world and determined to seek in silence, in complete silence, in a large house, bright and poor, where one feels the walls (and the sea on the horizon). Two having the desire of the two. The gazes that they bend on each other are distant and chaste, but constant. Every gesture of Catherine's has its correspondence in a gesture of Flore's; they think in the same way.

After several years of examples and proofs, Catherine and Flore no longer notice that they are almost a single person.

"In the time of Pierre Indemini, when I had to leave him," explains Catherine, "it was Flore I went back to first in Paris; I hardly paid any attention to her."

"I did not yet pay attention to you." It's Flore's voice, deeper, a beautiful contralto. The two of the them smile.

"She was leaving her sister. She had had enough of the profession she was in. She was as incisive as a little knife. Her life was no longer worth anything. She was poor . . . She wanted to compose music. She has done that, look now." (Catherine points to a score in manuscript on the piano.) "That's by her. And already Flore understood 'It' better than I did and would say to me: 'You are happy, Catherine.' Our friendship was beginning. But I thought only about myself, whereas she, in order to earn her living, was playing in a dance hall."

"But it's not the hell you say it is," says Flore. "It's very nice."

"Let me finish. After the misfortune at Garm . . . she arrived, accompanying Marguerite de Douxmaison. They were the ones who extracted me from the talons of justice in that place. Later she took me by the hand and said to me: 'Would you like it if we lived together? I will be nothing next to you. We will go without everything.'"

Flore Migett, in order to make Catherine be quiet, tried to close her mouth.

"Doesn't she look a little like me? Everyone says so."

"Everyone," Flore replies, "is almost no one."

Epilogue

Whoever enters a side box of the Opera during the performance of the first act if the lighting is dim will at first believe he is witnessing a singular event: this immense hall filled with motionless creatures, of which all the tiers appear faintly red-colored and as if transparently reflected in a brazier; against this background of characters marked by the tones of fabrics and skin, there are the women; behind, standing and all the same, as though petrified with astonishment, are the men, black and in shirtfronts. In this red fire, and all separated by the partitions that form recesses or protrusions, one has the vision of a "Last Judgment of High Society" in which all the weak figures would appear, paralyzed before the divine anger, ranked according to money and title.

At the same time that the music, with its broad musical hand, took hold of my spirit down to my farthest depths, effacing this worldly nightmare, I sensed immediately, though I had scarcely entered this performance of *Tristan,* an appeal, a desperate appeal reaching out to me from one of these figures.

Then, at the intermission, my eyes wandered over the balconies and the illuminated stairway. I felt at first that I was *not* looking at these balconies but that, mentally searching for Catherine, I was rereading in my mind the letters of a poster. Where? A poster along the way as I was coming to the Opera.

I returned to my seat and decided to find the hoped-for face. The theater was swarming with figures, rich, silky, under an indolent light; distant faces, infinitely removed, like other worlds. In the fourth box from mine toward the center, a woman could be seen from the back, wearing a dress of a delicate green and leaning over. Instantly I understood the meaning of the letters of the poster, which did not cause me any surprise. The figure leaning over in the silk dress of watery green interested me and attracted me much more. A fairly tall woman, and the first impression was that of character and dignity. As if this woman had felt my gaze, she covered her green dress with a full coat, also of silk but a metallic black. Now everything was black, the smooth, cropped head of hair, the coat, the attitude. Traces of gray in the hair adjoining the part. Part and hair of a softness so grave and so meditative that one was invincibly drawn and held. I noticed then the forehead, very well defined and closed, so to speak, against the outside. The word *pure* was inscribed on it. The nose . . . the skin . . . the ear, the little ear . . . But no, I did not want to believe my eyes, and that a woman still so young could be . . . But no, I said to myself, for if it is she—she is now close to forty.

The letters on the poster:

—————exclusive showing in Paris—————

RIVER OF FIRE

——————returning to the screen—————

—————Catharina—————

Catharina! It was the woman next to her who enabled me to recognize her at last. This woman looks like her, with truly gray hair and anxious features; I have found Flore Migett again.

I was in front of them when they came out of the box.

In Catherine Crachat's person there was a strange majesty, the majesty of a sleepwalker.

"It's you," she said. "How lovely. I am happy."

I looked at her attentively; no reality, no age. Not the slightest sign of fading. I expressed to her my emotion, my joy at seeing her again. Flore answered: "And so they still love us a little."

We went out onto the square, into the city. I was transported by happiness. I promised myself this time not to lose her again, whatever ruse she might employ to escape, and I saw a whole prospect of affection with both of them opening up. As we walked, I on the edge of the sidewalk, Catherine in the middle:

"Well, as you see, I've started it up again."

While she said these words she was gazing beyond things, beyond the depth of the night, at something that we others could not perceive. I noticed that Flore was helping her to walk and guiding her.

"Yes, yes!" I said with enthusiasm. "I only just found out about it, this very evening . . . "

"It was I who whispered it to you," said Catherine as though she were ashamed.

"And when was that?"

"Several months back," answered Flore.

"I'll go tomorrow! . . . "

"Don't go to it, don't go to it! I forbid you to," said Catherine violently. "It's not at all what I want to be doing. Don't go to it. It's shameful."

"Oh, Catherine, I so much admire you."

"My dear, you must be cold with me, gentle and cold. Ask Flore. The other day, near here, I caught sight of you. You didn't notice anything. All right, I said to myself, that's a sign; and I resolved to lose you again."

Her voice had a force so austere and almost wounding, so alienating, and contained so much inexplicable grief and joy coagulated together; I felt myself being led where she wanted, without putting up any resistance.

A car approached us. It was hers. She opened the door.

"May I see you again, Catherine?" I was imploring humbly.

"Yes, when you like."

"Where are you?"

"Nowhere. At the hotel. With our suitcases. Telephone us. Hôtel d'Astorg, rue d'Astorg."

"But we'll be leaving for London in ten days," Flore added. "Come in the next few days."

"Have you kept the country house?"

"No, it's been sold."

I said, more quietly, being so afraid of not seeing her again, "Are you at all happy, Catherine?"

"No. Why should I be, my friend? I am answering *in the sense of your question.*"

"And in another sense?"

"Sometimes very happy. Privileged."

"I understand you. What are you going to do?"

"I'm going to act, act. Act, naturally, until I drop."

She added very simply, "Nothing else but dying matters to me."

(I will see, I will know, I will find him again?)

I would have liked to kiss the earth behind the steps of that woman. She climbed into her car, and looked away.